This Book Belongs To:

_____

The Nights Before Christmas

The Nights Before Christmas

Illustrated by

Tony Ross

ANDERSEN PRESS

1

2

3

7

8

9

13

14

15

19

20

Clemens
U.S.A

21

4

5

6

10

11

12

16

17

18

22

23

24

This edition first published in 2018 by
Andersen Press Limited
20 Vauxhall Bridge Road
London SW1V 2SA
www.andersenpress.co.uk

2 4 6 8 10 9 7 5 3 1

This collection first published in 2014 in hardback by Andersen Press Ltd

'Professor Branestawm's Christmas Tree' by Norman Hunter from *The Peculiar Triumph
of Professor Branestawm* (Red Fox), copyright © Norman Hunter, 1970; reprinted by
permission of Random House Children's Books on behalf of the author's estate.

'In the Week When Christmas Comes' by Eleanor Farjeon from *Blackbird has Spoken*
(Macmillan), copyright © Eleanor Farjeon, 1927; reprinted by permission
of David Higham Associates on behalf of the poet's estate.

British Library Cataloguing in Publication Data available.

ISBN 978 1 78344 772 5

Printed and bound in China

Contents

A Message from the Illustrator

I always have and always will love Christmas. The Second World War raged through my early childhood but Christmases were still special and magical. In those years my family was joined for Christmas dinner by the airmen and glamorous land girls who were billeted with us. We had home-made decorations and crackers, a goose from a farmer friend, and all my new toys were wooden – my father told me that all the metal was being used to make Spitfires. As I've got older I may moan, like so many people, about how the spirit of Christmas has been spoilt by commerce, but no matter how greedy and aggressive retailers get, the old memories still creep through and win the day.

For me, so much of the excitement of Christmas comes from the anticipation. And that's why I wanted to illustrate this book – a collection of Christmas stories to help families count down the December nights until Christmas. When I was a child, Christmas started in our house just after bonfire night. School was decorated and the play was rehearsed; lessons became easier as the tension grew. Christmas Eve was my favourite, the busyness in the kitchen with my two grandmothers helping, the secrecy of my father and mother hiding things from me, my first sip of sherry, and knocks on the door. Then early to bed and the promise that Father Christmas would not come until I was asleep. There was some truth in that.

And for me now the best bit about Christmas isn't the day itself; it's still in the preparation – decorating the tree and bringing out the box of baubles that I greet like old friends. Whatever your own personal beliefs, customs and memories, I hope you will enjoy this book and that it will become part of your own family's tradition as you watch and wait for the wonder of Christmas.

Happy Christmas to all, and to all a good night.

NIGHT

1

A Visit from St Nicholas

By Clement Clarke Moore

A Visit from St Nicholas

By Clement Clarke Moore

'Twas the night before Christmas, when all through the house
Not a creature was stirring, not even a mouse.
The stockings were hung by the chimney with care,
In hopes that St Nicholas soon would be there.

The children were nestled all snug in their beds,
While visions of sugar-plums danced in their heads.
And mamma in her 'kerchief, and I in my cap,
Had just settled our brains for a long winter's nap –

A Visit from St Nicholas

When out on the lawn there arose such a clatter,
I sprang from the bed to see what was the matter.
Away to the window I flew like a flash,
Tore open the shutters and threw up the sash.

The moon on the breast of the new-fallen snow
Gave the lustre of midday to objects below;
When, what to my wondering eyes should appear,
But a miniature sleigh, and eight tiny reindeer.

With a little old driver, so lively and quick,
I knew in a moment it must be St Nick.
More rapid than eagles his coursers they came,
And he whistled, and shouted, and called them by name!

'Now, Dasher! Now, Dancer! Now, Prancer and Vixen!
On, Comet! On, Cupid! On, Donner and Blitzen!
To the top of the porch! To the top of the wall!
Now dash away! Dash away! Dash away all!'

As leaves that before the wild hurricane fly,
When they meet with an obstacle, mount to the sky;
So up to the house-top the coursers they flew,
With the sleigh full of toys, and St Nicholas too.

And then, in a twinkling, I heard on the roof
The prancing and pawing of each little hoof.
As I drew in my head, and was turning around,
Down the chimney St Nicholas came with a bound.

He was dressed all in fur, from his head to his foot,
And his clothes were all tarnished with ashes and soot.
A bundle of toys he had flung on his back,
And he looked like a pedlar, just opening his pack.

His eyes – how they twinkled! His dimples, how merry!
His cheeks were like roses, his nose like a cherry!
His droll little mouth was drawn up like a bow,
And the beard of his chin was as white as the snow.

The stump of a pipe he held tight in his teeth,
And the smoke it encircled his head like a wreath.
He had a broad face and a little round belly,
That shook when he laughed, like a bowlful of jelly!

He was chubby and plump, a right jolly old elf,
And I laughed when I saw him, in spite of myself!
A wink of his eye and a twist of his head
Soon gave me to know I had nothing to dread.

He spoke not a word, but went straight to his work,
And filled all the stockings, then turned with a jerk.
And laying his finger aside of his nose,
And giving a nod, up the chimney he rose!

He sprang to his sleigh, to his team gave a whistle,
And away they all flew like the down of a thistle.
But I heard him exclaim, 'ere he drove out of sight,
'Happy Christmas to all, and to all a good night!'

NIGHT

2

The Christmas Fairy
of Strasbourg

A German Folk Tale

Retold by J. Stirling Coyne

The Christmas Fairy of Strasbourg

A German Folk Tale
Retold by J. Stirling Coyne

Once, long ago, there lived near the ancient city of Strasbourg, on the River Rhine, a young and handsome count, whose name was Otto. As the years flew by he remained unwed, and never so much as cast a glance at the fair maidens of the country round; for this reason people began to call him 'Stone-Heart'.

It chanced that Count Otto, on one Christmas Eve, ordered that a great hunt should take place in the forest surrounding his castle. He and his guests and his many retainers rode forth, and the chase became more and more exciting. It led through thickets and over pathless tracts of forest, until at length Count Otto found himself separated from his companions.

He rode on by himself until he came to a spring of clear, bubbling water, known to the people around as the 'Fairy Well'. Here Count Otto dismounted. He bent over the spring and began to wash his hands in the sparkling tide, but to his wonder he found that though the weather was cold and frosty, the water was warm and delightfully caressing. He felt a glow of joy pass through his veins, and, as he plunged his hands deeper, he fancied that his right hand was grasped by another, soft and small, which gently slipped from his finger the gold ring he always wore. And, lo! when he drew out his hand, the gold ring was gone.

Full of wonder at this mysterious event, the count mounted his horse and returned to his castle, resolving in his mind that the very next day he would have the Fairy Well emptied by his servants.

He retired to his room, and, throwing himself just as he was upon his couch, tried to sleep, but the strangeness of the adventure kept him restless and wakeful.

Suddenly he heard the hoarse baying of the watch-hounds in the courtyard, and then the creaking of the drawbridge, as though it were being lowered. Then came to his ear the patter of many small feet on the stone staircase, and next he heard indistinctly the sound of light footsteps in the chamber adjoining his own.

Count Otto sprang from his couch, and as he did so there sounded a strain of delicious music and the door of his chamber was flung open. Hurrying into the next room, he found himself in the midst of numberless fairy beings, clad in gay and sparkling robes. They paid no heed to him, but began to dance, and laugh, and sing, to the sound of mysterious music.

In the centre of the apartment stood a splendid Christmas tree, the first ever seen in that country. Instead of toys and candles there hung on its lighted boughs diamond stars, pearl necklaces, bracelets of gold ornamented with collared jewels, aigrettes of rubies and sapphires, silken belts embroidered with Oriental pearls, and daggers mounted in gold and studded with the rarest gems. The whole tree swayed, sparkled, and glittered in the radiance of its many lights.

Count Otto stood speechless, gazing at all this wonder, when suddenly the fairies stopped dancing and fell back, to make room for a lady of dazzling beauty who came slowly towards him.

She wore on her raven-black hair a golden crown set with jewels. Her hair flowed down upon a robe of rosy satin and creamy velvet. She stretched out two small white hands to the count and addressed him in sweet, alluring tones:

'Dear Count Otto,' said she, 'I come to return your Christmas visit. I am Ernestine, the Queen of the Fairies. I bring you something you lost in the Fairy Well.'

And as she spoke she drew from her bosom a golden casket, set with diamonds, and placed it in his hands. He opened it eagerly and found within his lost gold ring.

Carried away by the wonder of it all, and overcome by an irresistible impulse, the count pressed the Fairy Ernestine to his heart, while she, holding him by the hand, drew him into the magic mazes of the dance. The mysterious music floated through the room, and the rest of that fairy company circled and whirled around the Fairy Queen and Count Otto, and then gradually dissolved into a mist of many colours, leaving the count and his beautiful guest alone.

Then the young man, forgetting all his former coldness towards the maidens of the country round about, fell on his knees before the fairy and besought her to become his bride. At last she consented, on the condition that he should never speak the word 'death' in her presence.

The next day the wedding of Count Otto and Ernestine, Queen of the Fairies, was celebrated with great pomp and magnificence, and the two continued to live happily for many years.

Now it happened on a time that the count and his fairy wife were to hunt in the forest around the castle. The horses were saddled and bridled. Standing at the door, the company waited, and the count paced the hall in great impatience, but still the Fairy Ernestine tarried long in her chamber. At length she appeared at the door of the hall, and the count addressed her in anger.

'You have kept us waiting so long,' he cried, 'that you would make a good messenger to send for Death!'

Scarcely had he spoken the forbidden and fatal word, when the fairy, uttering a wild cry, vanished from his sight. In vain Count Otto, overwhelmed with grief and remorse, searched the castle and the Fairy Well. No trace could he find of his beautiful lost wife but the imprint of her delicate hand set in the stone arch above the castle gate.

Years passed by, and the Fairy Ernestine did not return. The count continued to grieve. Every Christmas Eve he set up a lighted tree in the room where he had first met the fairy, hoping in vain that she would return to him.

Time passed and the count died. The castle fell into ruins. But to this day may be seen above the massive gate, deeply sunken in the stone arch, the impress of a small and delicate hand.

And such, say the good folk of Strasbourg, was the origin of the Christmas tree.

NIGHT

3

The Fir Tree

By Hans Christian Andersen

The Fir Tree

By Hans Christian Andersen

Far down in the forest, where the warm sun and the fresh air made a sweet resting place, grew a pretty little fir tree; and yet it was not happy, it wished so much to be tall like its companions – the pines and firs which grew around it. The sun shone, and the soft air fluttered its leaves, and the little peasant children passed by, prattling merrily, but the fir tree didn't pay them any attention.

Sometimes the children would bring a large basket of raspberries or strawberries and seat themselves near the fir tree, and say, 'Is it not a pretty little tree?' which made the tree feel more unhappy than before. And yet all this while the tree grew a notch or joint taller every year; you can tell the age of a fir tree by the number of joints in its stem.

Still, as it grew, it complained, 'Oh! how I wish I were as tall as the other trees. Then I would spread out my branches on every side, and my top would overlook the wide world. I should have the birds building their nests on my boughs, and when the wind blew, I should bow with stately dignity like my tall companions.'

The tree was so discontented that it took no pleasure in the warm sunshine, the birds, or the rosy clouds that floated over it morning and evening. Sometimes, in winter, when the snow lay white and glittering on the ground, a hare would come springing along, and jump right over

the little tree; and then how mortified it would feel!

Two winters passed, and when the third arrived, the tree had grown so tall that the hare was obliged to run around it. Yet it remained unsatisfied, and would exclaim, 'Oh, if I could but keep on growing tall and old! There is nothing else worth caring for in the world!'

In the autumn, as usual, the woodcutters came and cut down several of the tallest trees, and the young fir tree, which was now grown to its full height, shuddered as the noble trees fell to the earth with a crash. After the branches were lopped off, the trunks looked so slender and bare that they could scarcely be recognised. Then they were placed upon wagons, and drawn by horses out of the forest. Where were they going? What would become of them? The young fir tree wished very much to know, so in the spring, when the swallows and the storks came, it asked, 'Do you know where those trees were taken? Did you meet them?'

The swallows knew nothing, but the stork, after a little reflection, nodded his head, and said, 'Yes, I think I do. I met several new ships when I flew from Egypt, and they had fine masts that smelt like fir. I think these must have been the trees; I assure you they were stately, very stately.'

'Oh, how I wish I were tall enough to go on the sea,' said the fir tree. 'What is the sea, and what does it look like?'

'It would take too much time to explain,' said the stork, flying quickly away.

'Rejoice in your youth,' said the sunbeam. 'Rejoice in your fresh growth, and the young life that is in you.'

And the wind kissed the tree, and the dew watered it with tears, but the fir tree took no notice.

Christmas time drew near, and many young trees were cut down, some even smaller and younger than the fir tree, who enjoyed neither rest nor peace with longing to leave its forest home. These young trees, which were chosen for their beauty, kept their branches and were also laid on wagons and drawn by horses out of the forest.

'Where are they going?' asked the fir tree. 'They are not taller than I am: indeed, one is much less; and why are the branches not cut off? Where are they going?'

'We know, we know,' sang the sparrows. 'We have looked in at the windows of the houses in the town, and we know what is done with them. They are dressed up in the most splendid manner. We have seen them standing in the middle of a warm room, and adorned with all sorts of beautiful things – honey cakes, gilded apples, playthings, and many hundreds of wax candles.'

'And then . . . ?' asked the fir tree, trembling through all its branches. 'And then what happens?'

'We did not see any more,' said the sparrows, 'but this was enough for us.'

I wonder whether anything so brilliant will ever happen to me, thought the fir tree. It would be much better than crossing the sea. I long for it almost with pain. Oh, when will Christmas be here? I am now as tall and well grown as those which were taken away last year. Oh, that I were now laid on the wagon, or standing in the warm room, with all that brightness and splendour around me! Something better and more beautiful is to come after, or the trees would not be so decked out. Yes, what follows will be grander and more splendid. What can it be? I am weary with longing. I scarcely know how I feel.

'Rejoice with us,' said the air and the sunlight. 'Enjoy your own bright life in the fresh air.'

But the tree would not rejoice, though it grew taller every day; and, winter and summer, its dark green foliage might be seen in the forest, while passers-by would say, 'What a beautiful tree!'

A short time before Christmas, the discontented fir tree was the first to fall. As the axe cut through the tree, it fell with a groan to the earth, conscious of pain and faintness. It forgot all its anticipations of happiness, and felt sorrow at leaving its home in the forest. It knew that it would never again see its dear old companions, the trees, nor the little bushes and many-coloured flowers that had grown by its side; perhaps not even the birds. Neither was the journey at all pleasant. The tree first recovered itself while being unpacked in the courtyard of a house, with several other trees; and it heard a man say, 'We only want one, and this is the prettiest.'

Then came two servants in grand livery, and carried the fir tree into a large and beautiful apartment. On the walls hung pictures, and near the great stove stood great china vases, with lions on the lids. There were rocking chairs, silken sofas, large tables covered with pictures, books, and playthings, worth a great deal of money – at least, the children said so. Then the fir tree was placed in a large tub, full of sand; but green baize hung all around it, so that no one could see it was a tub, and it stood on a very handsome carpet.

How the fir tree trembled! 'What is going to happen to me now?' Some young ladies came, and the servants helped them to adorn the tree. On one branch they hung little bags cut out of coloured paper, and each bag was filled with sweetmeats; from other branches hung gilded apples and walnuts, as if they had grown there; and above, and all round, were hundreds of red, blue and white candles, which were fastened on the branches. Dolls, exactly like real babies, were placed under the green leaves – the tree had never seen such things before – and at the very top was fastened a glittering star, made of tinsel. Oh, it was very beautiful!

Oh, this evening the candles will be lighted, thought the tree, and then I shall know what else is going to happen. Will the trees of the forest come to see me? I wonder if the sparrows will peep in at the windows as they fly? Shall I grow faster here, and keep on all these ornaments summer and winter? But guessing was of very little use; it made its bark ache, and this pain is as bad for a slender fir tree as a headache is for us. At last the candles were lighted, and then what a glistening blaze of light the tree presented! It trembled with joy in all its branches, so that one of the candles fell among the green leaves and burned some of them.

'Help! Help!' exclaimed the young ladies, but there was no danger, for they quickly extinguished the fire. After this, the tree tried not to tremble at all, though the fire frightened it; it was so anxious not to hurt any of the beautiful ornaments, even while their brilliance dazzled it. And now the folding doors were thrown open, and a troop of children rushed in as if they intended to upset the tree; they were followed more silently by their elders. For a moment the little ones stood silent with astonishment, and then they shouted for joy, till the room rang, and they danced merrily around the tree, while one present after another was taken from it.

What are they doing? What will happen next? thought the fir.

At last the candles burned down to the branches and were put out. Then the children received permission to plunder the tree.

Oh, how they rushed upon it, till the branches cracked, and had the tree not been fastened with the glistening star to the ceiling, it would have been thrown down. The children then danced about with their pretty toys, and no one noticed the tree, except the children's maid who came and peeped among the branches to see if an apple or a fig had been forgotten.

'A story, a story,' cried the children, pulling a little fat man towards the tree.

'Now we shall be in the green shade,' said the man, as he seated himself under it, 'and the tree will have the pleasure of hearing also, but I shall only relate one story; what shall it be? Ivede-Avede, or Humpty Dumpty, who fell downstairs, but soon got up again, and at last married a princess.'

'Ivede-Avede,' cried some. 'Humpty Dumpty,' cried others, and there was a fine shouting and crying out. But the fir tree remained quite still, and thought to itself, Shall I have anything to do with all this? but it had already amused them as much as they wished. Then the old man told them the story of Humpty Dumpty and the children clapped their hands and cried, 'Tell another, tell another,' for they wanted to hear the story of 'Ivede-Avede'; but they only had 'Humpty Dumpty'. After this the fir tree became quite silent and thoughtful; never had the birds in the forest told such tales as 'Humpty Dumpty', who fell downstairs, and yet married a princess.

Ah, yes, so it happens in the world, thought the fir tree; it believed it all, because it was told by such a nice man. Ah well, it thought, who knows? Perhaps I may fall down too, and marry a princess. And it looked forward joyfully to the next evening, expecting to be again decked out with lights and playthings, gold and fruit. Tomorrow I will not tremble, it thought. I will enjoy all my splendour, and I will hear the story of Humpty Dumpty again, and perhaps Ivede-Avede. And the tree remained quiet and thoughtful all night.

In the morning the servants and the housemaid came in. Now, thought the fir, all my splendour is going to begin again. But they dragged it out of the room and upstairs to the attic, and threw it on the floor, in a dark corner, where no daylight shone, and there they left the fir tree.

What does this mean? thought the tree. What am I to do here? I can hear nothing in a place like this. And it had time enough to think, for days and nights passed and no one came near, and when at last somebody did come, it was only to put away large boxes in a corner. So the tree was completely hidden from sight as if it had never existed.

It is winter now, thought the tree. The ground is hard and covered with snow, so that people cannot plant me. I shall be sheltered here, I dare say, until spring comes. How thoughtful and kind everybody is to me! Still I wish this place were not so dark, as well as lonely, with not even a little hare to look at. How pleasant it was out in the forest while the snow lay on the ground, when the hare would run by, yes, and jump

over me too, although I did not like it then. Oh! it is terribly lonely here.

'Squeak, squeak,' said a little mouse, creeping cautiously towards the tree; then came another; and they both sniffed at the fir tree and crept between the branches.

'Oh, it is very cold,' said the little mouse, 'or else we should be so comfortable here, shouldn't we, you old fir tree?'

'I am not old,' said the fir tree, 'there are many who are older than I am.'

'Where do you come from? And what do you know?' asked the mice, who were full of curiosity. 'Have you seen the most beautiful places in the world, and can you tell us all about them? And have you been in the storeroom, where cheeses lie on the shelf, and hams hang from the ceiling? One can run about on tallow candles there, and go in thin and come out fat.'

'I know nothing of that place,' said the fir tree, 'but I know the wood where the sun shines and the birds sing.' And then the tree told the little mice all about its youth. They had never heard such an account in their lives; and after they had listened to it attentively, they said, 'What a number of things you have seen! You must have been very happy.'

'Happy?' exclaimed the fir tree, and then as it reflected upon what it had been telling them, it said, 'Ah, yes! After all, those were happy days.' But when it went on and related all about Christmas Eve, and how it had been dressed up with cakes and lights, the mice said, 'How happy you must have been, you old fir tree.'

'I am not old at all,' replied the tree. 'I only came from the forest this winter. I am now checked in my growth.'

'What splendid stories you can relate,' said the little mice. And the next night four other mice came with them to hear what the tree had to tell. The more it talked the more it remembered, and then it thought to itself, Those were happy days, but they may come again. Humpty Dumpty fell downstairs, and yet he married the princess; perhaps I may marry a princess too. And the fir tree thought of the pretty little birch tree that grew in the forest, which seemed like a real beautiful princess.

'Who is Humpty Dumpty?' asked the little mice. And then the tree related the whole story; it could remember every single word, and the little mice were so delighted with it that they were ready to jump to the top of the tree. The next night a great many more mice made their appearance, and on Sunday two rats came with them; but they said it was not a pretty story at all, and the little mice were very sorry, for it made them also think less of it.

'Do you know only one story?' asked the rats.

'Only one,' replied the fir tree. 'I heard it on the happiest evening of my life; but I did not know I was so happy at the time.'

'We think it is a very miserable story,' said the rats. 'Don't you know any story about bacon, or tallow in the storeroom?'

'No,' replied the tree.

'Many thanks to you then,' replied the rats, and they marched off.

The little mice also kept away after this, and the tree sighed, and said, 'It was very pleasant when the merry little mice sat round me and listened while I talked. Now that is all passed too. However, I shall consider myself happy when someone comes to take me out of this place.'

But would this ever happen? Yes; one morning people came to clear out the attic, the boxes were packed away and the tree was pulled out of the corner and thrown roughly on the attic floor; then the servant dragged it out upon the staircase where the daylight shone. 'Now life is beginning again,' said the tree, rejoicing in the sunshine and fresh air. Then it was carried downstairs and taken into the courtyard so quickly that it forgot to think of itself and could only look about; there was so much to be seen. The courtyard was close to a garden, where everything looked blooming.

Fresh and fragrant roses hung over the little palings. The linden trees were in blossom, while the swallows flew here and there, crying, 'Twit, twit, twit, my mate is coming' – but it was not the fir tree they meant.

'Now I shall live,' cried the tree, joyfully spreading out its branches; but alas they were all withered and yellow, and it lay in a corner among weeds and nettles. The star of gold paper still stuck in the top of the tree and glittered in the sunshine.

In the same courtyard two of the merry children were playing who had danced around the tree at Christmas and had been so happy. The youngest saw the gilded star, and ran and pulled it off the tree. 'Look what is sticking to the ugly old fir tree,' said the child, treading on the branches till they crackled under his boots. And the tree saw all the fresh bright flowers in the garden, and then looked at itself, and wished it had remained in the dark corner of the attic. It thought of its fresh youth in the forest, of the merry Christmas evening, and of the little mice who had listened to the story of 'Humpty Dumpty'. 'Past! past!' said the old tree; 'Oh, had I but enjoyed myself while I could have done so! But now it is too late.'

Then a lad came and chopped the tree into small pieces, till a large bundle lay in a heap on the ground. The pieces were placed on a bonfire, and they quickly blazed up brightly, while the tree sighed so deeply that each sigh was like a pistol shot. Then the children, who were at play, came and seated themselves in front of the fire, and looked at it and cried, 'Pop, pop.' But at each 'pop', which was a deep sigh, the tree was thinking of a summer day in the forest, and of Christmas evening, and of 'Humpty Dumpty', the only story it had ever heard or knew how to relate, till at last it was consumed. The boys still played in the garden, and the youngest wore on his breast the golden star with which the tree had been adorned during the happiest evening of its existence.

Now all was past; the tree's life was past, and the story also – for all stories must come to an end at last.

NIGHT

4

The Nativity

From the King James Bible

The Birth of Jesus

And it came to pass in those days, that there went out a decree from Caesar Augustus, that all the world should be taxed. (And this taxing was first made when Cyrenius was governor of Syria.)

And all went to be taxed, every one into his own city. And Joseph also went up from Galilee, out of the city of Nazareth, into Judea, unto the city of David, which is called Bethlehem (because he was of the house and lineage of David) to be taxed with Mary his espoused wife, being great with child.

And so it was, that, while they were there, the days were accomplished that she should be delivered.

And she brought forth her firstborn son, and wrapped him in swaddling clothes, and laid him in a manger; because there was no room for them in the inn.

Luke 2: 1-7

The Shepherds and the Angels

*A*nd there were in the same country shepherds abiding in the field, keeping watch over their flock by night.

And, lo, the angel of the Lord came upon them, and the glory of the Lord shone round about them; and they were sore afraid.

And the angel said unto them, 'Fear not: for, behold, I bring you good tidings of great joy, which shall be to all people.

'For unto you is born this day in the city of David a Saviour, which is Christ the Lord.

'And this shall be a sign unto you; Ye shall find the babe wrapped in swaddling clothes, lying in a manger.'

And suddenly there was with the angel a multitude of the heavenly host praising God, and saying, *Glory to God in the highest, and on earth peace, good will towards men.*

And it came to pass, as the angels were gone away from them into heaven, the shepherds said one to another, 'Let us now go even unto Bethlehem, and see this thing which is come to pass, which the Lord hath made known unto us.'

And they came with haste, and found Mary and Joseph, and the babe lying in a manger.

Luke 2: 8-20

The Visit of the Magi

Now, when Jesus was born in Bethlehem of Judaea in the days of Herod the king, behold, there came wise men from the east to Jerusalem, saying, 'Where is he that is born King of the Jews? for we have seen his star in the east, and are come to worship him.'

When Herod the king had heard these things, he was troubled, and all Jerusalem with him.

And when he had gathered all the chief priests and scribes of the people together, he demanded of them where Christ should be born.

And they said unto him, 'In Bethlehem of Judaea: for thus it is written by the prophet, and thou Bethlehem, in the land of Juda, art not the least among the princes of Juda: for out of thee shall come a Governor, that shall rule my people Israel.'

Then Herod, when he had privily called the wise men, enquired of them diligently what time the star appeared. And he sent them to Bethlehem, and said, 'Go and search diligently for the young child; and when ye have found him, bring me word again, that I may come and worship him also.'

When they had heard the king, they departed; and, lo, the star, which they saw in the east, went before them, till it came and stood over where the young child was. When they saw the star, they rejoiced with exceeding great joy. And when they were come into the house, they saw the young child with Mary his mother, and fell down, and worshipped him: and when they had opened their treasures, they presented unto him gifts; gold, and frankincense, and myrrh.

Matthew 2: 1-11

NIGHT

5

Papa Panov's Special Christmas

Retold by Leo Tolstoy

Papa Panov's Special Christmas

Retold by Leo Tolstoy

It was Christmas Eve, and although it was still afternoon, lights had begun to appear in the shops and houses of the little Russian village, for the short winter day was nearly over. Excited children scurried indoors and now only muffled sounds of chatter and laughter escaped from closed shutters.

Old Papa Panov, the village shoemaker, stepped outside his shop to take one last look around. The sounds of happiness, the bright lights and the faint but delicious smells of Christmas cooking reminded him of past Christmas times when his wife had still been alive and his own children little. Now they had gone. His usually cheerful face, with the little laughter wrinkles behind the round steel spectacles, looked sad now. But he went back indoors with a firm step, put up the shutters and set a pot of coffee to heat on the stove. Then, with a sigh, he settled in his big armchair.

Papa Panov did not often read, but tonight he pulled down the big old family Bible and, slowly tracing the lines with one forefinger, he read again the Christmas story. He read how Mary and Joseph, tired by their journey to Bethlehem, found no room for them at the inn, so that Mary's little baby was born in the cowshed.

'Oh dear, oh dear!' exclaimed Papa Panov, 'if only they had come here! I would have given them my bed and I could have covered the baby with my patchwork quilt to keep him warm.'

He read on about the wise men who had come to see the baby Jesus, bringing him splendid gifts. Papa Panov's face fell. I have no gift that I could give him, he thought sadly.

Then his face brightened. He put down the Bible, got up and stretched his long arms to the shelf high up in his little room. He took down a small, dusty box and opened it. Inside was a perfect pair of tiny leather shoes. Papa Panov smiled with satisfaction. Yes, they were as good as he had remembered – the best shoes he had ever made. 'I should give him those,' he decided, as he gently put them away and sat down again.

He was feeling tired now, and the further he read the sleepier he became. The print began to dance before his eyes so that he closed them, just for a minute. In no time at all Papa Panov was fast asleep.

And as he slept he dreamed. He dreamed that someone was in his room and he knew at once, as one does in dreams, who the person was. It was Jesus.

'You have been wishing that you could see me, Papa Panov,' he said kindly, 'then look for me tomorrow. It will be Christmas Day and I will visit you. But look carefully, for I shall not tell you who I am.'

When at last Papa Panov awoke, the bells were ringing out and a thin light was filtering through the shutters. 'Bless my soul!' said Papa Panov. 'It's Christmas Day!'

He stood up and stretched himself for he was rather stiff. Then his face filled with happiness as he remembered his dream. This would be a very special Christmas after all, for Jesus was coming to visit him. How would he look? Would he be a little baby, as at that first Christmas? Would he be a grown man, a carpenter – or the great King that he is, God's Son? He must watch carefully the whole day through so that he recognised him however he came.

Papa Panov put on a special pot of coffee for his Christmas breakfast, took down the shutters and looked out of the window. The street was deserted, no one was stirring yet. No one except the road sweeper. He looked as miserable and dirty as ever, and well he might! Whoever wanted to work on Christmas Day – and in the raw cold and bitter freezing mist of such a morning?

Papa Panov opened the shop door, letting in a thin stream of cold air. 'Come in!' he shouted across the street cheerily. 'Come in and have some hot coffee to keep out the cold!'

The sweeper looked up, scarcely able to believe his ears. He was only too glad to put down his broom and come into the warm room. His old clothes steamed gently in the heat of the stove and he clasped both red hands round the comforting warm mug as he drank.

Papa Panov watched him with satisfaction, but every now and then his eyes strayed to the window. It would never do to miss his special visitor.

'Expecting someone?' the sweeper asked at last. So Papa Panov told him about his dream.

'Well, I hope he comes,' the sweeper said. 'You've given me a bit of Christmas cheer I never expected to have. I'd say you deserve to have your dream come true.' And he actually smiled.

When he had gone, Papa Panov put on cabbage soup for his dinner, then went to the door again, scanning the street. He saw no one. But he was mistaken. Someone was coming.

The girl walked so slowly and quietly, hugging the walls of shops and houses, that it was a while before he noticed her. She looked very tired and she was carrying something. As she drew nearer he could see that it was a baby, wrapped in a thin shawl. There was such sadness in her face and in the pinched little face of the baby, that Papa Panov's heart went out to them.

'Won't you come in?' he called, stepping outside to meet them. 'You both need a warm by the fire and a rest.'

The young mother let him shepherd her indoors and to the comfort of the armchair. She gave a big sigh of relief.

'I'll warm some milk for the baby,' Papa Panov said. 'I've had children of my own – I can feed her for you.' He took the milk from the stove and carefully fed the baby from a spoon, warming her tiny feet by the stove at the same time.

'She needs shoes,' the cobbler said.

But the girl replied, 'I can't afford shoes, I've got no husband to bring home money. I'm on my way to the next village to get work.'

A sudden thought flashed through Papa Panov's mind. He remembered the little shoes he had looked at last night. But he had been keeping those for Jesus. He looked again at the cold little feet and made up his mind.

'Try these on her,' he said, handing the baby and the shoes to the mother. The beautiful little shoes were a perfect fit. The girl smiled happily and the baby gurgled with pleasure.

'You have been so kind to us,' the girl said, when she got up with her baby to go. 'May all your Christmas wishes come true!'

But Papa Panov was beginning to wonder if his very special Christmas wish would come true. Perhaps he had missed his visitor? He looked anxiously up and down the street. There were plenty of people about but they were all faces that he recognised. There were neighbours going to call on their families. They nodded and smiled and wished him Happy Christmas! Or beggars – and Papa Panov hurried indoors to fetch them hot soup and a generous hunk of bread, hurrying out again in case he missed the Important Stranger.

All too soon the winter dusk fell. When Papa Panov next went to the door and strained his eyes, he could no longer make out the passers-by. Most were home and indoors by now anyway. He walked slowly back into his room at last, put up the shutters and sat down wearily in his armchair.

So it had been just a dream after all. Jesus had not come.

Then all at once he knew that he was no longer alone in the room.

This was not a dream for he was wide awake. At first he seemed to see before his eyes the long stream of people who had come to him that day. He saw again the old road sweeper, the young mother and her baby and the beggars he had fed. As they passed, each whispered, 'Didn't you see me, Papa Panov?'

'Who are you?' he called out, bewildered.

Then another voice answered him. It was the voice from his dream – the voice of Jesus.

'I was hungry and you fed me,' he said. 'I was naked and you clothed me. I was cold and you warmed me. I came to you today in every one of those you helped and welcomed.'

Then all was quiet and still. Only the sound of the big clock ticking. A great peace and happiness seemed to fill the room, overflowing Papa Panov's heart until he wanted to burst out singing and laughing and dancing with joy.

'So he did come after all!' was all that he said.

NIGHT

6

Good King Wenceslas

By John Mason Neale

Good King Wenceslas

By John Mason Neale

Good King Wenceslas looked out
On the feast of Stephen
When the snow lay round about
Deep and crisp and even
Brightly shone the moon that night
Though the frost was cruel
When a poor man came in sight
Gath'ring winter fuel.

'Hither, page, and stand by me
If thou know'st it, telling
Yonder peasant, who is he?
Where and what his dwelling?'
'Sire, he lives a good league hence
Underneath the mountain
Right against the forest fence
By St Agnes' fountain.'

'Bring me flesh and bring me wine
Bring me pine logs hither
Thou and I will see him dine
When we bear him thither.'
Page and monarch forth they went
Forth they went together
Through the rude wind's wild lament
And the bitter weather.

'Sire, the night is darker now
And the wind blows stronger
Fails my heart, I know not how,
I can go no longer.'
'Mark my footsteps, my good page
Tread thou in them boldly
Thou shalt find the winter's rage
Freeze thy blood less coldly.'

In his master's steps he trod
Where the snow lay dinted
Heat was in the very sod
Which the saint had printed
Therefore, Christian men, be sure
Wealth or rank possessing
Ye who now will bless the poor
Shall yourselves find blessing.

NIGHT

7

The Elves and the Shoemaker

By the Brothers Grimm

The Elves and the Shoemaker

By the Brothers Grimm

A shoemaker, by no fault of his own, had become so poor that at last he had nothing left but leather for one pair of shoes. So in the evening, he cut out the shoes, which he wished to begin to make the next morning, and as he had a good conscience, he lay down quietly in his bed, commended himself to God and fell asleep. In the morning, after he had said his prayers, and was just going to sit down to work, the two shoes stood quite finished on his table. He was astounded! He took the shoes in his hands to observe them closer. They were so neatly made that there was not one bad stitch in them, just as if they were intended as a masterpiece.

Soon after, a buyer came in, and as the shoes pleased him so well, he paid more for them than was customary, and, with the money, the shoemaker was able to purchase leather for two pairs of shoes. He cut them out at night, and next morning was about to set to work with fresh courage; but he had no need to do so, for, when he got up, they were already made, and soon buyers gave him money enough to buy leather for four pairs of shoes. The following morning, too, he found the four pairs made; and so it went on – what he cut out in the evening was finished by the morning, so that he soon had his honest independence again, and at last became a wealthy man.

Now it befell that one evening not long before Christmas, when the man had been cutting out, he said to his wife, before going to bed, 'What do you think if we were to stay up tonight to see who it is that lends us this helping hand?' The woman liked the idea, and lighted a candle, and then they hid themselves in a corner of the room, behind some hanging clothes, and watched. When it was midnight, two pretty little naked men came, sat down by the shoemaker's table, took all the work which was cut out before them and began to stitch and sew and hammer so skilfully and so quickly with their little fingers that the astonished shoemaker couldn't turn away his eyes. They did not stop until all was done and stood finished on the table; and then they ran quickly away.

Next morning the woman said, 'The little men have made us rich, and we really must show that we are grateful for it. They run about so, and have nothing on, and must be cold. I'll tell you what I'll do: I will make them little shirts, and coats, and vests, and trousers, and knit both of them a pair of stockings, and you, too, will make them two little pairs of shoes.' The man said, 'I shall be very glad to do it,' and one night, when everything was ready, they laid their presents all together on the table instead of the cut-out work, and then concealed themselves to see how the little men would behave. At midnight the men came bounding in, and wanted to get to work at once, but they did not find any leather cut out, but only the pretty little articles of clothing. At first they were astonished, and then they showed intense delight. They dressed themselves with the greatest rapidity, putting the pretty clothes on, and singing,

> *'Now we are boys so fine to see,*
> *Why should we longer cobblers be?'*

Then they danced and skipped and leaped over chairs and benches. At last they danced out of doors. From that time forth they came no more, but as long as the shoemaker lived all went well with him, and all his undertakings prospered.

NIGHT

8

An extract from

A Christmas Carol

By Charles Dickens

An extract from

A Christmas Carol

By Charles Dickens

Once upon a time – of all the good days in the year, on Christmas Eve – old Ebenezer Scrooge sat busy in his counting house. It was cold, bleak, biting weather: foggy withal: and he could hear the people in the court outside go wheezing up and down, beating their hands upon their breasts and stamping their feet upon the pavement stones to warm them. The city clocks had only just gone three, but it was quite dark already – it had not been light all day: and candles were flaring in the windows of the neighbouring offices, like ruddy smears upon the palpable brown air. The fog came pouring in at every chink and keyhole, and was so dense without, that although the court was of the narrowest, the houses opposite were mere phantoms. To see the dingy cloud come drooping down, obscuring everything, one might have thought that Nature lived hard by, and was brewing on a large scale.

The door of Scrooge's counting house was open that he might keep his eye upon his clerk, who in a dismal little cell beyond, a sort of tank, was copying letters. Scrooge had a very small fire, but the clerk's fire was so very much smaller that it looked like one coal. But he couldn't replenish it, for Scrooge kept the coalbox in his own room; and so surely as the clerk came in with the shovel, the master predicted that it would be necessary for them to part. Wherefore the clerk put on his white comforter, and tried to warm himself at the candle; in which effort, not being a man of a strong imagination, he failed.

'A merry Christmas, Uncle! God save you!' cried a cheerful voice. It was the voice of Scrooge's nephew, who came upon him so quickly that this was the first intimation he had of his approach.

'Bah!' said Scrooge. 'Humbug!'

He had so heated himself with rapid walking in the fog and frost, this nephew of Scrooge's, that he was all in a glow; his face was ruddy and handsome; his eyes sparkled, and his breath smoked again.

'Christmas a humbug, Uncle!' said Scrooge's nephew. 'You don't mean that, I am sure.'

'I do,' said Scrooge. 'Merry Christmas? What right have you to be merry? What reason have you to be merry? You're poor enough.'

'Come, then,' returned the nephew gaily. 'What right have you to be dismal? What reason have you to be morose? You're rich enough.'

Scrooge, having no better answer ready on the spur of the moment, said 'Bah!' again; and followed it up with 'Humbug.'

'Don't be cross, Uncle!' said the nephew.

'What else can I be,' returned the uncle, 'when I live in such a world of fools as this? Merry Christmas? Out upon merry Christmas! What's Christmas time to you but a time for paying bills without money; a time for finding yourself a year older, but not an hour richer; a time for balancing your books and having every item in 'em through a round dozen of months presented dead against you? If I could work my will,' said Scrooge indignantly, 'every idiot who goes about with "Merry Christmas" on his lips should be boiled with his own pudding and buried with a stake of holly through his heart. He should!'

'Uncle!' pleaded the nephew.

'Nephew!' returned the uncle sternly. 'Keep Christmas in your own way, and let me keep it in mine.'

'Keep it?' repeated Scrooge's nephew. 'But you don't keep it.'

'Let me leave it alone then,' said Scrooge. 'Much good may it do you! Much good it has ever done you!'

'There are many things from which I might have derived good, by which I have not profited, I dare say,' returned the nephew. 'Christmas among the rest. But I am sure I have always thought of Christmas time, when it has come round – apart from the veneration due to its sacred name and origin, if anything belonging to it can be apart from that – as a good time: a kind, forgiving, charitable, pleasant time; the only time I know of, in the long calendar of the year, when men and women seem by one consent to open their shut-up hearts freely, and to think of people below them as if they really were fellow-passengers to the grave, and not another race of creatures bound on other journeys. And therefore, Uncle, though it has never put a scrap of gold or silver in my pocket, I believe that it has done me good, and will do me good; and I say, God bless it!'

The clerk in the tank involuntarily applauded. Becoming immediately sensible of the impropriety, he poked the fire, and extinguished the last frail spark for ever.

'Let me hear another sound from you,' said Scrooge, 'and you'll keep your Christmas by losing your situation. You're quite a powerful

speaker, sir,' he added, turning to his nephew. 'I wonder you don't go into Parliament.'

'Don't be angry, Uncle. Come! Dine with us tomorrow.'

Scrooge said that he would see him – yes, indeed he did. He went the whole length of the expression, and said that he would see him in that extremity first.

'But why?' cried Scrooge's nephew. 'Why?'

'Why did you get married?' said Scrooge.

'Because I fell in love.'

'Because you fell in love!' growled Scrooge, as if that were the only one thing in the world more ridiculous than a merry Christmas. 'Good afternoon!'

'Nay, Uncle, but you never came to see me before that happened. Why give it as a reason for not coming now?'

'Good afternoon,' said Scrooge.

'I want nothing from you; I ask nothing of you; why cannot we be friends?'

'Good afternoon,' said Scrooge.

'I am sorry, with all my heart, to find you so resolute. We have never had any quarrel to which I have been a party. But I have made the trial in homage to Christmas, and I'll keep my Christmas humour to the last. So A Merry Christmas, Uncle!'

'Good afternoon,' said Scrooge.

'And A Happy New Year!'

'Good afternoon!' said Scrooge.

His nephew left the room without an angry word, notwithstanding. He stopped at the outer door to bestow the greetings of the season on the clerk, who cold as he was, was warmer than Scrooge; for he returned them cordially.

Why the Evergreen Trees Never Lose their Leaves

By Florence Holbrook

Why the Evergreen Trees Never Lose their Leaves

By Florence Holbrook

Winter was coming, and the birds had flown far to the south, where the air was warm and they could find berries to eat. One little bird had broken its wing and could not fly with the others. It was alone in the cold world of frost and snow. The forest looked warm, and it made its way to the trees as well as it could, to ask for help.

First it came to a birch tree. 'Beautiful birch tree,' it said, 'my wing is broken, and my friends have flown away. May I live among your branches till they come back to me?'

'No, indeed,' answered the birch tree, drawing her fair green leaves away. 'We of the great forest have our own birds to help. I can do nothing for you.'

'The birch is not very strong,' said the little bird to itself, 'and it might be that she could not hold me easily. I will ask the oak.' So the bird said, 'Great oak tree, you are so strong. Will you not let me live on your boughs till my friends come back in the springtime?'

'In the springtime!' cried the oak. 'That is a long way off. How do I know what you might do in all that time? Birds are always looking for something to eat, and you might even eat up some of my acorns.'

It may be that the willow will be kind to me, thought the bird, and it said, 'Gentle willow, my wing is broken, and I could not fly to the south with the other birds. May I live on your branches till the springtime?'

The willow did not look gentle then, for she drew herself up proudly and said, 'Indeed, I do not know you, and we willows never talk to people whom we do not know. Very likely there are trees somewhere that will take in strange birds. Leave me at once.'

The poor little bird did not know what to do. Its wing was not yet strong, but it began to fly away as well as it could. Before it had gone far a voice was heard. 'Little bird,' it said, 'where are you going?'

'Indeed, I do not know,' answered the bird sadly. 'I am very cold.'

'Come right here then,' said the friendly spruce tree, for it was her voice that had called. 'You shall live on my warmest branch all winter if you choose.'

'Will you really let me?' asked the little bird eagerly.

'Indeed I will,' answered the kind-hearted spruce tree. 'If your friends have flown away, it is time for the trees to help you. Here is the branch where my leaves are thickest and softest.'

'My branches are not very thick,' said the friendly pine tree, 'but I am big and strong, and I can keep the North Wind from you and the spruce.'

'I can help too,' said a little juniper tree. 'I can give you berries all winter long, and every bird knows that juniper berries are good.'

So the spruce gave the lonely little bird a home; the pine kept the cold North Wind away from it; and the juniper gave it berries to eat. The other trees looked on and talked together wisely.

'I would not have strange birds on my boughs,' said the birch.

'I shall not give my acorns away for anyone,' said the oak.

'I never have anything to do with strangers,' said the willow, and the three trees drew their leaves closely about them.

In the morning all those shining, green leaves lay on the ground, for a cold North Wind had come in the night, and every leaf that it touched fell from the tree.

'May I touch every leaf in the forest?' asked the wind in its frolic.

'No,' said the Frost King. 'The trees that have been kind to the little bird with the broken wing may keep their leaves.'

This is why the leaves of the spruce, the pine and the juniper are always green.

NIGHT

10

An extract from

The Wind in the Willows

By Kenneth Grahame

The Wind in the Willows

By Kenneth Grahame

After a long day's outing with Otter, hunting and exploring on the wide uplands, Rat and Mole made their way to Rat's home, River Bank, where a warm dinner awaited them on this cold winter's night. As they journeyed on in the darkness, Mole caught a whiff of his own home, which he had left long ago. He continued on after his friend, but he could not contain his sorrow for long; shortly he broke into sobs and confessed to Rat that they had passed by Mole's long-abandoned home, to which he desperately longed to return.

'Hang River Bank, and supper too!' said the Rat heartily. 'I tell you, I'm going to find this place now, if I stay out all night. So cheer up, old chap, and take my arm, and we'll very soon be back there again.'

Still snuffling, pleading and reluctant, Mole suffered himself to be dragged back along the road by his imperious companion, who by a flow of cheerful talk and anecdote endeavoured to beguile his spirits back and make the weary way seem shorter. When at last it seemed to the Rat that they must be nearing that part of the road where the Mole had been 'held up', he said, 'Now, no more talking. Business! Use your nose, and give your mind to it.'

They moved on in silence for some little way, when suddenly the Rat was conscious, through his arm that was linked in Mole's, of a faint sort of electric thrill that was passing down that animal's body. Instantly he disengaged himself, fell back a pace and waited, all attention.

The signals were coming through!

Mole stood a moment rigid, while his uplifted nose, quivering slightly, felt the air.

Then a short, quick run forward – a fault – a check – a try back; and then a slow, steady, confident advance.

The Rat, much excited, kept close to his heels as the Mole, with something of the air of a sleepwalker, crossed a dry ditch, scrambled through a hedge and nosed his way over a field open and trackless and bare in the faint starlight.

Suddenly, without giving warning, he dived; but the Rat was on the alert, and promptly followed him down the tunnel to which his unerring nose had faithfully led him.

It was close and airless, and the earthy smell was strong, and it seemed a long time to Rat ere the passage ended and he could stand erect and stretch and shake himself. The Mole struck a match, and by its light the Rat saw that they were standing in an open space, neatly swept and sanded underfoot, and directly facing them was Mole's little front door, with 'Mole End' painted, in Gothic lettering, over the bell-pull at the side.

Mole reached down a lantern from a nail on the wall and lit it, and the Rat, looking round him, saw that they were in a sort of forecourt. A garden seat stood on one side of the door, and on the other a roller; for the Mole, who was a tidy animal when at home, could not stand having his ground kicked up by other animals into little runs that ended in earth-heaps. On the walls hung wire baskets with ferns in them, alternating with brackets carrying plaster statuary – Garibaldi, and the infant Samuel, and Queen Victoria, and other heroes of modern Italy. Down on one side of the forecourt ran a skittle alley, with benches

along it and little wooden tables marked with rings that hinted at beer mugs. In the middle was a small round pond containing goldfish and surrounded by a cockleshell border. Out of the centre of the pond rose a fanciful erection clothed in more cockleshells and topped by a large silvered glass ball that reflected everything all wrong and had a very pleasing effect.

Mole's face beamed at the sight of all these objects so dear to him, and he hurried Rat through the door, lit a lamp in the hall and took one glance round his old home. He saw the dust lying thick on everything, saw the cheerless, deserted look of the long-neglected house, and its narrow, meagre dimensions, its worn and shabby contents – and collapsed again on a hall chair, his nose to his paws. 'Oh, Ratty!' he cried dismally, 'Why ever did I do it? Why did I bring you to this poor, cold little place, on a night like this, when you might have been at River Bank by this time, toasting your toes before a blazing fire, with all your own nice things about you!'

The Rat paid no heed to his doleful self-reproaches. He was running here and there, opening doors, inspecting rooms and cupboards, and lighting lamps and candles and sticking them up everywhere. 'What a capital little house this is!' he called out cheerily. 'So compact! So well planned! Everything here and everything in its place! We'll make a jolly night of it. The first thing we want is a good fire; I'll see to that – I always know where to find things. So this is the parlour? Splendid! Your own idea, those little sleeping-bunks in the wall? Capital! Now, I'll fetch the wood and the coals, and you get a duster, Mole – you'll find one in the drawer of the kitchen table – and try and smarten things up a bit. Bustle about, old chap!'

Encouraged by his inspiriting companion, the Mole roused himself and dusted and polished with energy and heartiness, while the Rat, running to and fro with armfuls of fuel, soon had a cheerful blaze roaring up the chimney. He hailed the Mole to come and warm himself; but Mole promptly had another fit of the blues, dropping down on a couch in dark despair and burying his face in his duster. 'Rat,' he moaned, 'how about your supper, you poor, cold, hungry, weary animal? I've nothing to give you – nothing – not a crumb!'

'What a fellow you are for giving in!' said the Rat reproachfully. 'Why, only just now I saw a sardine-opener on the kitchen dresser, quite distinctly; and everybody knows that means there are sardines about somewhere in the neighbourhood. Rouse yourself! Pull yourself together, and come with me and forage.'

They went and foraged accordingly, hunting through every cupboard and turning out every drawer. The result was not so very depressing after all, though of course it might have been better; a tin of sardines – a box of captain's biscuits, nearly full – and a German sausage encased in silver paper.

'There's a banquet for you!' observed the Rat, as he arranged the table. 'I know some animals who would give their ears to be sitting down to supper with us tonight!'

'No bread!' groaned the Mole dolorously; 'no butter, no—'

'No pâté de foie gras, no champagne!' continued the Rat, grinning. 'And that reminds me – what's that little door at the end of the passage? Your cellar, of course! Every luxury in this house! Just you wait a minute.'

He made for the cellar door, and presently reappeared, somewhat dusty, with a bottle of beer in each paw and another under each arm, 'Self-indulgent beggar you seem to be, Mole,' he observed. 'Deny yourself nothing. This is really the jolliest little place I ever was in. Now, wherever did you pick up those prints? Make the place look so home-like, they do. No wonder you're so fond of it, Mole. Tell us all about it, and how you came to make it what it is.'

Then, while the Rat busied himself fetching plates, and knives and forks, and mustard which he mixed in an egg cup, the Mole, his bosom still heaving with the stress of his recent emotion, related – somewhat shyly at first, but with more freedom as he warmed to his subject – how this was planned, and how that was thought out, and how this was got through a windfall from an aunt, and that was a wonderful find and a bargain, and this other thing was bought out of laborious savings and a certain amount of 'going without'. His spirits finally quite restored, he must needs go and caress his possessions, and take a lamp and show off their points to his visitor and expatiate on them, quite forgetful of the supper they both so much needed, Rat, who was desperately hungry but strove to conceal it, nodding seriously, examining with a puckered brow, and saying, 'wonderful', and 'most remarkable', at intervals, when the chance for an observation was given him.

At last the Rat succeeded in decoying him to the table, and had just got seriously to work with the sardine-opener when sounds were heard from the forecourt without – sounds like the scuffling of small feet in the gravel and a confused murmur of tiny voices, while broken sentences reached them – 'Now, all in a line – hold the lantern up a bit, Tommy – clear your throats first – no coughing after I say one, two, three. – Where's young Bill? – Here, come on, do, we're all a-waiting—'

'What's up?' inquired the Rat, pausing in his labours.

'I think it must be the fieldmice,' replied the Mole, with a touch of pride in his manner. 'They go round carol-singing regularly at this time of the year. They're quite an institution in these parts. And they never pass me over – they come to Mole End last of all; and I used to give them hot drinks, and supper too sometimes, when I could afford it. It will be like old times to hear them again.'

'Let's have a look at them!' cried the Rat, jumping up and running to the door.

It was a pretty sight, and a seasonable one, that met their eyes when they flung the door open. In the forecourt, lit by the dim rays of a horn lantern, some eight or ten little fieldmice stood in a semicircle, red worsted comforters round their throats, their forepaws thrust deep into their pockets, their feet jigging for warmth. With bright beady eyes they glanced shyly at each other, sniggering a little, sniffing and applying coat sleeves a good deal. As the door opened, one of the elder ones that carried the lantern was just saying, 'Now then, one, two, three!' and forthwith their shrill little voices uprose on the air, singing one of the old-time carols that their forefathers composed in fields that were fallow and held by frost, or when snow-bound in chimney corners, and handed down to be sung in the miry street to lamp-lit windows at Yule-time.

Villagers all, this frosty tide,
Let your doors swing open wide,
Though wind may follow, and snow beside,
Yet draw us in by your fire to bide;
Joy shall be yours in the morning!
Here we stand in the cold and the sleet,
Blowing fingers and stamping feet,
Come from far away you to greet –
You by the fire and we in the street –
Bidding you joy in the morning!
For ere one half of the night was gone,
Sudden a star has led us on,
Raining bliss and benison –
Bliss tomorrow and more anon,
Joy for every morning!

Goodman Joseph toiled through the snow –
Saw the star o'er a stable low;
Mary she might not further go –
Welcome thatch, and litter below!
Joy was hers in the morning!
And then they heard the angels tell
'Who were the first to cry Nowell?
Animals all, as it befell,
In the stable where they did dwell!
Joy shall be theirs in the morning!'

The voices ceased, the singers, bashful but smiling, exchanged sidelong glances, and silence succeeded – but for a moment only.

Then, from up above and far away, down the tunnel they had so lately travelled was borne to their ears in a faint musical hum the sound of distant bells ringing a joyful and clangorous peal.

'Very well sung, boys!' cried the Rat heartily. 'And now come along in, all of you, and warm yourselves by the fire, and have something hot!'

'Yes, come along, fieldmice,' cried the Mole eagerly. 'This is quite like old times! Shut the door after you. Pull up that settle to the fire. Now, you just wait a minute, while we . . . Oh, Ratty!' he cried in despair, plumping down on a seat, with tears impending. 'Whatever are we doing? We've nothing to give them!'

'You leave all that to me,' said the masterful Rat. 'Here, you with the lantern! Come over this way. I want to talk to you. Now, tell me, are there any shops open at this hour of the night?'

'Why, certainly, sir,' replied the fieldmouse respectfully. 'At this time of the year our shops keep open to all sorts of hours.'

'Then look here!' said the Rat. 'You go off at once, you and your lantern, and you get me—'

Here much muttered conversation ensued, and the Mole only heard bits of it, such as – 'Fresh, mind! – no, a pound of that will do – see you get Buggins's, for I won't have any other – no, only the best – if you can't get it there, try somewhere else – yes, of course, home-made, no tinned stuff – well then, do the best you can!' Finally, there was a chink of coin passing from paw to paw, the fieldmouse was provided with an ample basket for his purchases, and off he hurried, he and his lantern.

The rest of the fieldmice, perched in a row on the settle, their small legs swinging, gave themselves up to enjoyment of the fire, and toasted their chilblains till they tingled; while the Mole, failing to draw them into easy conversation, plunged into family history and made each of them recite the names of his numerous brothers, who were too young, it appeared, to be allowed to go out a-carolling this year, but looked

forward very shortly to winning the parental consent.

The Rat, meanwhile, was busy examining the label on one of the beer bottles. 'I perceive this to be Old Burton,' he remarked approvingly. 'Sensible Mole! The very thing! Now we shall be able to mull some ale! Get the things ready, Mole, while I draw the corks.'

It did not take long to prepare the brew and thrust the tin heater well into the red heart of the fire; and soon every fieldmouse was sipping and coughing and choking (for a little mulled ale goes a long way) and wiping his eyes and laughing and forgetting he had ever been cold in all his life.

'They act plays too, these fellows,' the Mole explained to the Rat. 'Make them up all by themselves, and act them afterwards. And very well they do it too! They gave us a capital one last year, about a fieldmouse who was captured at sea by a Barbary corsair, and made to row in a galley; and when he escaped and got home again, his lady-love had gone into a convent. Here, you! You were in it, I remember. Get up and recite a bit.'

The fieldmouse addressed got up on his legs, giggled shyly, looked round the room, and remained absolutely tongue-tied. His comrades cheered him on, Mole coaxed and encouraged him, and the Rat went so far as to take him by the shoulders and shake him; but nothing could overcome his stage fright. They were all busily engaged on him like watermen applying the Royal Humane Society's regulations to a case of long submersion, when the latch clicked, the door opened and the fieldmouse with the lantern reappeared, staggering under the weight of his basket.

There was no more talk of play-acting once the very real and solid contents of the basket had been tumbled out on the table. Under the generalship of Rat, everybody was set to do something or to fetch something. In a very few minutes supper was ready, and Mole, as he took the head of the table in a sort of a dream, saw a lately barren board set thick with savoury comforts; saw his little friends' faces brighten and beam as they fell to without delay; and then let himself loose – for he was famished indeed – on the provender so magically provided, thinking what a happy homecoming this had turned out, after all. As they ate, they talked of old times, and the fieldmice gave him the local gossip up to date, and answered as well as they could the hundred questions he had to ask them. The Rat said little or nothing, only taking care that each guest had what he wanted, and plenty of it, and that Mole had no trouble or anxiety about anything.

They clattered off at last, very grateful and showering wishes of the season, with their jacket pockets stuffed with remembrances for the small brothers and sisters at home. When the door had closed on the last of them and the chink of the lanterns had died away, Mole and Rat kicked the fire up, drew their chairs in, brewed themselves a last nightcap of mulled ale and discussed the events of the long day. At last the Rat, with a tremendous yawn, said, 'Mole, old chap, I'm ready to drop. Sleepy is simply not the word. That your own bunk over on that side? Very well then, I'll take this. What a ripping little house this is! Everything so handy!'

He clambered into his bunk and rolled himself well up in the blankets, and slumber gathered him forthwith, as a swathe of barley is folded into the arms of the reaping machine.

The weary Mole also was glad to turn in without delay, and soon had his head on his pillow, in great joy and contentment. But ere he closed his eyes he let them wander round his old room, mellow in the glow of the firelight that played or rested on familiar and friendly things which had long been unconsciously a part of him, and now smilingly received him back, without rancour. He was now in just the frame of mind that the tactful Rat had quietly worked to bring about in him. He saw clearly how plain and simple – how narrow, even – it all was; but clearly, too, how much it all meant to him, and the special value of some such anchorage in one's existence. He did not at all want to abandon the new life and its splendid spaces, to turn his back on sun and air and all they offered him and creep home and stay there; the upper world was all too strong, it called to him still, even down there, and he knew he must return to the larger stage. But it was good to think he had this to come back to; this place which was all his own, these things which were so glad to see him again and could always be counted upon for the same simple welcome.

NIGHT

11

The Snow Queen

By Hans Christian Andersen

The Snow Queen

By Hans Christian Andersen

The Story of the Mirror and Its Fragments

There was once a very wicked hobgoblin; he was one of the very worst, for he was a real demon. One day, when he was in a merry mood for he had just made a mirror which made everything good or beautiful that was reflected in it almost shrink to nothing, while everything that was worthless and bad seemed increased in size and worse than ever. In this mirror the most lovely landscapes appeared like boiled spinach, and the most beautiful people became hideous and looked as if they stood on

their heads and had no bodies. Their features were so distorted that no one could recognise them, and even one freckle on the face appeared to spread over the whole of the nose and mouth. The demon thought this was very amusing and he laughed at his cunning invention.

All the goblins who went to the demon's school – for he kept a school – talked everywhere of the wonders they had seen, and declared that people could now, for the first time, see what the world and mankind were really like. They carried the mirror about everywhere, till at last there was not a land nor a people who had not been looked at through this distorted looking glass. They wanted even to fly with it up to heaven to see the angels, but the higher they flew the more slippery the glass became, and they could scarcely hold it, till at last it slipped from their hands, fell to the earth and was broken into millions of pieces.

But now the mirror caused more unhappiness than ever, for some of the fragments were smaller than a grain of sand, and they flew about the world into every country. When one of these tiny atoms flew into a person's eye, it stuck there unknown to him, and from that moment he saw everything the wrong way and only had eyes for what was evil and corrupt. For even the smallest fragment retained the same power which had belonged to the whole mirror. Some people even got a fragment of the mirror in their hearts, and this was disastrous, for their hearts became cold like a lump of ice. A few of the pieces were so large that they could be used as windowpanes; it would have been a sad thing to look at our friends through them. Other pieces were made into spectacles; this was dreadful for those who wore them, for they could see nothing either rightly or justly. At all this the wicked demon laughed till his sides shook – it tickled him so to see the mischief he had done. There were still a number of these little fragments of glass floating about in the air, and now you shall hear what happened with one of them.

A Little Boy and a Little Girl

In a large town, so full of houses and people that there was not room for everybody to have a little garden, and many people had to be satisfied with a few flowers in flowerpots, there lived two poor children who had a garden something larger and better than a few flowerpots. They were not brother and sister, but they loved each other almost as much as if they had been.

Their parents lived opposite to each other in two garrets, where the roofs of neighbouring houses projected out towards each other and the gutter ran between them. In each house was a little window, so that anyone could step across the gutter from one window to the other. The parents of these children each had a large wooden box in which they grew kitchen herbs, and a little rosebush in each box, which grew splendidly. Now after a while the parents decided to place these two boxes across the water pipe, so that they reached from one window to the other and looked like two banks of flowers. Sweetpeas drooped over the boxes,

and the rosebushes shot forth long branches, which were trained round the windows and clustered together almost like a triumphal arch of leaves and flowers. The boxes were very high, and the children knew they must not climb upon them without permission, but they were often, however, allowed to step out together and sit upon their little stools under the rosebushes, or play quietly.

In winter all this pleasure came to an end, for the windows were sometimes quite frozen over. But then they would warm copper pennies on the stove, and hold the warm pennies against the frozen pane; there would be very soon a little round hole through which they could peep, and the soft bright eyes of the little boy and girl would beam through the hole at each window as they looked at each other.

Their names were Kay and Gerda. In summer they could be together with one jump from the window, but in winter they had to go up and down the long staircase and out through the snow before they could meet.

'See, there are the white bees swarming,' said Kay's old grandmother one day when it was snowing.

'Have they a queen bee?' asked the little boy, for he knew that the real bees had a queen.

'They have,' said the grandmother. 'She is flying there where the swarm is thickest. She is the largest of them all, and never remains on the earth, but flies up to the dark clouds. Often at midnight she flies through the streets of the town, and looks in at the windows; then the ice freezes on the panes into wonderful shapes, that look like flowers and castles.'

'Yes, I have seen them,' said both the children, and they knew it must be true.

'Can the Snow Queen come in here?' asked the little girl.

'If she comes in,' said the boy, 'I'll put her on the stove and then she'll melt.'

Then the grandmother smoothed his hair and told him some more tales.

One evening, when little Kay was at home, half undressed, he climbed onto a chair by the window and peeped out through the little hole. A few flakes of snow were falling, and one of them, rather larger than the rest, landed on the edge of one of the flower boxes. This snowflake grew larger and larger, till at last it became the figure of a woman, dressed in the finest robe made from millions of starry snowflakes linked together. She was fair and beautiful, but made of ice – shining and glittering ice. Her eyes sparkled like bright stars, but there was neither peace nor rest in their glance. She nodded towards the window and waved her hand. The little boy was frightened and sprang from the chair to hide; at the same moment it seemed as if a large bird flew by the window.

On the following day there was a clear frost, and very soon came the spring. The sun shone; the young green leaves burst forth; the swallows built their nests; windows were opened, and the children sat once more in the garden on the roof, high above all the other rooms. How beautiful the roses blossomed this summer. The little girl had learned a hymn in which roses were spoken of, and then she thought of their own roses, and she sang the hymn to the little boy, and he sang too:

'Roses bloom and cease to be,
But we shall the Christ-child see.'

Then the little ones held each other by the hand, and kissed the roses, and looked at the bright sunshine, and spoke to it as if the Christ-child were there. Those were splendid summer days. How beautiful and fresh it was out among the rosebushes, which looked as though they would never stop blooming.

One day Kay and Gerda were sitting looking at a book full of pictures of animals and birds, when suddenly Kay said, 'Oh, something has struck my heart!' and soon after, 'There is something in my eye.'

The little girl put her arm round his neck, and looked into his eye, but she could see nothing.

'I think it is gone,' he said. But it was not gone; it was one of those bits of the magic mirror, of which we have spoken – the wicked glass which made everything great and good appear small and ugly, while all that was wicked and bad became more visible, and every little fault could be plainly seen. Poor little Kay also had a small grain in his heart, which very quickly turned to a lump of ice. He no longer felt the pain, but the glass was there still.

'Why do you cry?' he said at last. 'It makes you look ugly. There is nothing the matter with me now. Oh, see!' he cried suddenly, 'That rose has a worm in it, and this one is quite crooked. After all they are ugly roses, just like the box in which they stand,' and then he kicked the boxes with his foot, and pulled off the two roses.

'Kay, what are you doing?' cried the little girl; and then, when he saw how frightened she was, he tore off another rose and jumped through his own window, away from little Gerda.

When she afterwards brought out the picture book, he called it a baby's book, and when Grandmother told any stories, he would interrupt her with 'but'; or, when he could manage it, he would get behind her chair, put on a pair of spectacles, and imitate her very cleverly, to make people laugh. By and by he began to mimic everybody in the street.

All that was peculiar or disagreeable in a person he would imitate directly, and people said, 'That boy will be very clever; he has a remarkable genius.' But it was the piece of glass in his eye, and the coldness in his heart, that made him act like this. He would even tease little Gerda, who loved him with all her heart.

His games too were quite different; they were not so childish. One winter's day, when it snowed, he brought out a magnifying glass, and held it against his coat where the snowflakes fell upon it. 'Look in this glass, Gerda,' said he; and she saw how every flake of snow was magnified and looked like a beautiful flower or a glittering star. 'Is it not clever?' said Kay. 'And much more interesting than looking at real flowers. There is not a single fault in it, and the snowflakes are quite perfect till they begin to melt.'

Soon after Kay came in with large thick gloves, and with his sledge at his back. He called upstairs to Gerda, 'I've got to leave to go into the great square, where the other boys play and ride.' And away he went.

In the great square, the boldest among the boys would often tie their sledges to the country people's carts, and go with them a good way. This was great fun. But while they were all amusing themselves, and Kay with them, a great sledge came by; it was painted white, and in it sat someone wrapped in a rough white fur, and wearing a white cap. The sledge drove twice around the square, and Kay fastened his own little sledge to it, so that when it went away, he followed with it. It went faster and faster right through the next street, and then the person who drove turned round and nodded pleasantly to Kay, just as if they were acquainted with each other, but whenever Kay wished to loosen his little sledge the driver nodded again, so Kay sat still, and they drove out through the town gate. Then the snow began to fall so heavily that the little boy could not see a hand's breadth before him, but still they drove on; then he suddenly loosened the cord so that the large sled might go on without him, but it was of no use, his little carriage held fast, and away they went like the wind. Then he called out loudly, but nobody heard him, while the snow beat upon him, and the sledge flew onwards. Every now and then it gave a jump as if it were going over hedges and ditches. The boy was frightened, and tried to say a prayer, but he could remember nothing but the multiplication table.

The snowflakes became larger and larger, till they appeared like great white birds. All at once they parted, the great sledge stopped, and the person who had driven it rose up from the seat. The fur and the cap, which were made entirely of snow, fell off, and he saw a lady, tall and white. It was the Snow Queen.

'We have driven well,' said she, 'but why do you tremble? Here, creep into my warm fur.' Then she seated him beside her in the sledge, and as she wrapped the fur round him he felt as if he were sinking into a snow drift.

'Are you still cold?' she asked, as she kissed him on the forehead. The kiss was colder than ice; it went quite through to his heart, which was already almost a lump of ice; he felt as if he were going to die, but only for a moment; he soon seemed quite well again, and did not notice the cold around him.

My sledge! Don't forget my sledge, was his first thought, and then he looked and saw that it was bound fast to one of the white birds, which flew behind him with the sledge at its back. The Snow Queen kissed little Kay again, and by this time he had forgotten little Gerda, his grandmother and all at home.

'Now you must have no more kisses,' she said, 'or I should kiss you to death.'

Kay looked at her, and saw that she was so beautiful he could not imagine a more lovely and intelligent face. She did not now seem to be made of ice, as when he had seen her through his window and she had nodded to him. In his eyes she was perfect, and he did not feel at all afraid. He told her how good he was at mental arithmetic, even fractions, and that he knew the number of square miles and the number of inhabitants in the country. And she always smiled so that he thought he did not know enough yet, and she looked round the vast expanse as she flew higher and higher with him upon a black cloud, while the storm blew and howled as if it were singing old songs. They flew over woods and lakes, over sea and land; below them roared the wild wind; the wolves howled and the snow crackled; over them flew the black screaming crows, and above all shone the moon, clear and bright – and so Kay passed through the long winter's night, and by day he slept at the feet of the Snow Queen.

The Flower Garden of the Woman Who Could Conjure

But how was little Gerda when Kay never returned? What had become of him no one knew, nor could anyone give the slightest information, except the boys who said that he had tied his sledge to another very large one, which had driven out of the town gate. Nobody knew where it went and many tears were shed for him. Little Gerda wept and wept because everyone said he must be drowned in the river. Oh, indeed those long winter days were very dreary. But at last spring came, with warm sunshine.

'Kay is dead and gone,' said little Gerda.

'I don't believe it,' said the sunshine.

'He is dead and gone,' she said to the sparrows.

'We don't believe it,' they replied; and at last little Gerda began to doubt it herself. 'I will put on my new red shoes,' she said one morning, 'those that Kay has never seen, and then I will go down to the river and ask for him.'

It was quite early when she kissed her old grandmother, who was still asleep; then she put on her red shoes, and went quite alone out of the town gates towards the river. 'Is it true that you have taken my little friend away from me?' she said to the river. 'I will give you my red shoes if you will give him back to me.'

And it seemed as if the waves nodded to her in a strange manner. Then she took off her red shoes, which she liked better than anything else, and threw them both into the river, but they fell near the bank, and the little waves carried them back to the land, just as if the river

would not take from her what she loved best, because it could not give her back little Kay. But she thought the shoes had not been thrown out far enough. So she crept into a boat that lay among the reeds and threw the shoes again from the further end of the boat into the water. But it was not fastened and her movement sent it gliding away from the land. When she saw this she hurried to reach the end of the boat, but before she could do so it was more than a yard from the bank, and drifting away faster than ever.

Then little Gerda was very frightened, and began to cry, but no one heard her except the sparrows, and they could not carry her to land, but they flew along by the shore, and sang, as if to comfort her, 'Here we are! Here we are!' The boat floated with the stream.

Perhaps the river will carry me to little Kay, thought Gerda, and then she became more cheerful, and raised her head, and looked at the beautiful green banks; and so the boat sailed on for hours. At last she came to a large cherry orchard, in which stood a small red house with strange red and blue windows and a thatched roof. Outside were two wooden soldiers who stood to attention as she sailed past.

Gerda called out to them, for she thought they were alive, but of course they did not answer; and as the boat drifted nearer to the shore, she saw what they really were. Then Gerda called still louder, and an old woman came out of the house, leaning on a crutch. She wore a large hat with the prettiest flowers painted on it.

'You poor little child,' said the old woman, 'the river has brought you a long way.' And she walked into the water, seized the boat with her crutch, drew it to land and lifted Gerda out. And Gerda was glad to feel herself on dry ground, although she was rather afraid of the strange old woman.

'Come and tell me who you are,' said she, 'and how came you here.'

So Gerda told her everything, while the old woman shook her head, and said, 'Hem-hem'; and when she had finished, Gerda asked if she had seen little Kay, and the old woman told her he had not passed by that way, but he was sure to come soon. So she told Gerda not to be sad, but to taste the cherries and look at the flowers; they were better than any picture book, for each of them could tell a story.

Then she took Gerda by the hand and led her into the little house, and the old woman closed the door. On the table stood beautiful cherries, and Gerda was allowed to eat as many as she wanted. While she was eating them the old woman combed out her long hair with a golden comb.

'I have long been wishing for a dear little girl like you,' said the old woman, 'and now you must stay with me, and see how happily we shall live together.' And while she went on combing little Gerda's hair, Gerda thought less and less about her little Kay, for the old woman was an enchantress and she wanted to keep Gerda. So she went into the garden and stretched out her crutch towards all the rose trees, beautiful though they were, and they immediately sank into the dark earth, so that no one could tell where they had once stood. The old woman was afraid that if little Gerda saw roses she would think of those at home, and then remember little Kay, and run away. Then she took Gerda into the flower garden. How fragrant and beautiful it was! Flowers of every season grew there. Gerda jumped for joy, and played till the sun went down behind the tall cherry trees; then she slept in a little bed with red silk pillows embroidered with coloured violets and dreamed sweetly.

The next day, and for many days after, Gerda played with the flowers in the warm sunshine. She knew every flower, and yet, although there were so many of them, it seemed as if one were missing, but which it was she could not tell. One day, however, as she sat looking at the old woman's hat with the painted flowers on it, she saw that the prettiest of them all was a rose. The old woman had forgotten to take it from her hat when she made all the roses sink into the earth.

'Why are there no roses here?' cried Gerda; and she ran out into the garden, and examined all the beds, and searched and searched. There was not one to be found. Then she sat down and wept, and her tears fell just on the place where one of the rose trees had been. The warm tears moistened the earth, and the rose tree sprouted up at once. Gerda embraced it and kissed the roses, and immediately remembered little Kay.

'Oh, how could I have stayed so long?' said the girl. 'I wanted to look for Kay. Do you know where he is?' she asked the roses; 'do you think he is dead?'

And the roses answered, 'No, he is not dead. We have been in the ground where all the dead lie; but Kay is not there.'

'Thank you,' said little Gerda, and then she went to the other flowers, and looked into their little cups, and asked, 'Do you know where little Kay is?' But each flower, as it stood in the sunshine, dreamed only of its own little fairy tale of history. Not one knew anything of Kay.

Then she ran to the other end of the garden. The door was fastened, but she pressed against the rusty latch, and it gave way. The door sprang open, and little Gerda ran out with bare feet into the wide world. She looked back three times, but no one seemed to be following her. At last she could run no longer, so she sat down to rest on a great stone, and when she looked round she saw that the summer was over, and autumn very far advanced. She had known nothing of this in the beautiful garden, where the sun shone and the flowers grew all the year round.

'Oh, how I have wasted my time!' said little Gerda. 'It is autumn. I must not rest any longer.' And she rose up to go on. But her little feet were wounded and sore, and everything around her looked so cold and bleak. The long willow leaves were quite yellow. The dewdrops fell like water, leaf after leaf dropped from the trees, the sloethorn alone still bore fruit, but the sloes were sour. Oh, how dark and weary the whole world appeared!

The Prince and Princess

Gerda had to rest again. Suddenly she saw a great crow come hopping across the snow towards her. He stood looking at her for some time, and then he wagged his head and said, 'Caw, caw; good-day, good-day.' Then he asked her where she was going all alone in the wide world.

Gerda told him the whole story of her life and adventures, and asked him if he had seen little Kay.

The crow nodded his head very gravely, and said, 'Perhaps I have – it may be.'

'Do you think you have?' cried little Gerda, and she kissed the crow, and hugged him almost to death with joy.

'Gently, gently,' said the crow. 'I believe I know. I think it may be little Kay; but he has certainly forgotten you by this time for the princess.'

'Does he live with a princess?' asked Gerda.

'Yes, listen,' replied the crow, 'but it is so difficult to speak your language. If you understand the crows' language then I can explain it better. Do you?'

'No, I have never learned it,' said Gerda, 'but my grandmother understands it, and used to speak it to me. I wish I had learned it.'

'It does not matter,' answered the crow; 'I will explain as well as I can.' And he told her what he had heard. 'In this kingdom where we now are,' he said, 'there lives a very clever princess. A short time ago, as she was sitting on her throne, she began to sing a song which commences in these words:

'Why should I not be married?'

'"Why not indeed?" said she, and so she determined to marry if she could find a husband who knew what to say when he was spoken to, and not one who could only look grand, for that was so tiresome. You may believe that every word I tell you is true,' said the crow, 'for I have a tame sweetheart who goes freely about the palace, and she told me all this.'

Of course his sweetheart was a crow, for 'birds of a feather flock together', and one crow always chooses another crow.

'Newspapers were published immediately, with a border of hearts, and the initials of the princess among them. They proclaimed that every young man who was handsome was free to visit the castle and speak with the princess; and those who could reply loud enough to be heard when spoken to were to make themselves quite at home at the palace; but the one who spoke best would be chosen as a husband for the princess. Yes, yes, you may believe me, it is all as true as I sit here,' said the crow. 'The people came in crowds, but no one succeeded either on the first or second day. They could all speak very well while they were outside in the streets, but when they entered the palace gates, and saw the guards in silver uniforms, and the footmen in their golden livery on the staircase, and the great halls lighted up, they became quite speechless. And when they stood before the throne on which the princess sat, they could do nothing but repeat the last words she had said; and she had no particular wish to hear her own words over again. It was just as if they had all been struck dumb while they were in the palace, for they did not recover themselves nor speak till they got back again into the street. There was quite a long line of them reaching from the town gate to the palace. I went myself to see them,' said the crow.

'But Kay! Tell me about little Kay!' said Gerda, 'was he among the crowd?'

'Stop a bit, we are just coming to him. It was on the third day, there came marching cheerfully along to the palace a little personage, without horses or carriage, his eyes sparkling like yours; he had beautiful long hair, but his clothes were very poor.'

'That was Kay!' said Gerda joyfully. 'Oh, then I have found him.' And she clapped her hands.

'He had a little knapsack on his back,' added the crow.

'No, it must have been his sledge,' said Gerda; 'for he went away with it.'

'It may have been so,' said the crow; 'I did not look at it very closely. But I heard from my sweetheart that he passed through the palace gates, saw the guards in their silver uniform, and the servants in their liveries of gold on the stairs, but he was not in the least confused. 'It must be very tiresome to stand on the stairs,' he said. 'I prefer to go in.' The rooms were blazing with light and his boots creaked loudly as he walked, and yet he was not at all uneasy.'

'It must be Kay,' said Gerda. 'I know he had new boots. I have heard them creak in Grandmother's room.'

'They really did creak,' said the crow, 'yet he went boldly up to the princess herself, who was sitting on a pearl as large as a spinning wheel. The young man spoke just as well as I do, when I speak the crows' language. He was quite free and agreeable and said he had not come to woo the princess, but to hear her wisdom; and he was as pleased with her as she was with him.'

'Oh, certainly that was Kay,' said Gerda. 'He was so clever; he could do arithmetic in his head and fractions. Oh, will you take me to the palace?'

'It is very easy to ask that,' replied the crow, 'but how are we to manage it? However, I will speak about it to my tame sweetheart, and ask her advice; for I must tell you it will be very difficult to gain permission for a little girl like you to enter the palace.'

'Oh, yes; but I shall gain permission easily,' said Gerda, 'for when Kay hears that I am here, he will come out and fetch me in immediately.'

'Wait for me here by the palings,' said the crow, wagging his head as he flew away.

It was late in the evening before the crow returned. 'Caw, caw,' he said, 'my sweetheart sends you greeting, and here is a little roll which she took from the kitchen for you; there is plenty of bread there, and she thinks you must be hungry. It is not possible for you to enter the palace by the front entrance. The guards in silver uniform and the servants in gold livery would not allow it. But do not cry, we will manage to get you in; my sweetheart knows a little back staircase that leads to the sleeping apartments, and she knows where to find the key.'

So they went into the garden through the great avenue, where the leaves were falling one after another, and they could see the light in the palace being put out in the same manner. And the crow led little Gerda to the back door, which stood ajar. Oh, how little Gerda's heart beat with anxiety and longing; it was just as if she were going to do something wrong, and yet she only wanted to know where little Kay was. It must be him, she thought. She would see if his smile was the same. He would certainly be glad to see her, and to hear what a long distance she had come for his sake, and to know how everyone at home missed him.

They were now on the stairs, and in a small closet at the top a lamp was burning. In the middle of the floor stood the tame crow, turning her head from side to side, and gazing at Gerda, who curtsied as her grandmother had taught her to do.

'My betrothed has spoken so very highly of you, my little lady,' said the tame crow; 'your life history is very touching. If you will take the lamp I will walk before you. We will go straight along this way, then we shall meet no one.'

They now came into the first room. Its walls were hung with rose-coloured satin, embroidered with flowers. Some dreams flitted by them but so quickly Gerda could not see them. Each room that they went through was more splendid than the last, it was enough to bewilder anyone. At length they reached a bedroom. The ceiling was like a great palm tree, with glass leaves of the most costly crystal, and over the centre of the floor two beds, each resembling a lily, hung from a stem of gold.

One, in which the princess lay, was white, the other was red; and in this Gerda hoped to find little Kay. She pushed one of the red leaves aside, and saw a little brown neck. Oh, that must be Kay! She called his name out quite loud, and held the lamp over him. The dreams rushed by. He woke, and turned his head round, but it was not little Kay!

Then the princess peeped out of her white-lily bed, and asked what was the matter. Then little Gerda wept and told her story, and all that the crows had done to help her.

'You poor child,' said the prince and princess; then they praised the crows, and said they were not angry for what they had done, but that it must not happen again, and this time they should be rewarded.

'Would you like to have your freedom,' asked the princess, 'or would you prefer to be raised to the position of court crows, with all that is left in the kitchen for yourselves?'

Then both the crows bowed, and chose the appointment at court, for they thought of their old age, and said it would be so comfortable to be provided for. And then the prince got out of his bed, and gave it up to Gerda and she lay down.

The following day she was dressed from head to foot in silk and velvet, and they invited her to stay at the palace for a few days, and enjoy herself, but she only begged for a pair of boots, and a little carriage, and a horse to draw it, so that she might go into the wide world to seek for Kay. And she obtained, not only boots, but also a muff, and she was neatly dressed; and when she was ready to go, there, at the door, she found a coach made of pure gold and the coachman, footman and outriders all wearing golden crowns on their heads. The prince and princess

themselves helped her into the coach, and wished her success. The forest crow, who was now married, accompanied her for the first three miles; he sat by Gerda's side, as he could not bear riding backwards. The tame crow stood in the doorway flapping her wings. She could not go with them, because she had been suffering from a headache ever since the new appointment, no doubt from eating too much. The coach was well stored with sweet cakes, and under the seat were fruit and gingerbread nuts. 'Farewell, farewell,' cried the prince and princess, and little Gerda wept, and the crow wept; and then, after a few miles, the crow also said, 'Farewell,' and this was the saddest parting. However, he flew to a tree, and stood flapping his black wings as long as he could see the coach, which glittered in the bright sunshine.

The Little Robber-Girl

The coach drove on through a thick forest, where it lighted up the way like a torch, and attracted the eyes of some robbers.

'It is gold! It is gold!' they cried, rushing forward and seizing the horses. Then they struck the outriders, the coachman and the footman dead, and pulled little Gerda out of the carriage.

'She is fat and pretty, and she has been fed with the kernels of nuts,' said the old robber-woman, who had a long beard and eyebrows that hung over her eyes. 'She is as good as a little lamb; how nice she will taste!' and as she said this, she drew forth a shining knife, that glittered horribly. 'Oh!' screamed the old woman the same moment, for her own daughter had jumped on her back and bitten her in the ear. She was a wild and naughty girl, and the mother called her an ugly thing, and had not time to kill Gerda.

'She shall play with me,' said the little robber-girl; 'she shall give me her muff and her pretty dress, and sleep with me in my bed.' And then she bit her mother again, and made her spring in the air and jump about; and all the robbers laughed, and said, 'See how she is dancing with her daughter.'

'I will have a ride in the coach,' said the little robber-girl; and she would have her own way, for she was so self-willed and spoiled.

She and Gerda seated themselves in the coach and drove away, over stumps and stones, into the depths of the forest. The little robber-girl was about the same size as Gerda, but stronger; she had broader shoulders and a darker skin; her eyes were quite black, and she had a mournful look. She clasped little Gerda round the waist and said, 'They shall not kill you as long as you don't make us vexed with you. I suppose you are a princess.'

'No,' said Gerda; and then she told her all her history, and how fond she was of little Kay.

The robber-girl looked earnestly at her, nodded her head slightly, and said, 'They shan't kill you, even if I do get angry with you; for I will do it myself.' And then she wiped Gerda's eyes, and stuck her own hands in the beautiful muff which was so soft and warm.

The coach stopped in the courtyard of the robbers' castle, the walls of which were cracked from top to bottom. Ravens and crows flew in and out of the holes and crevices, while great bulldogs, either of which looked as if it could swallow a man, were jumping about, but they were not allowed to bark.

In the large and smoky hall a bright fire was burning on the stone floor. There was no chimney, so the smoke went up to the ceiling, and found a way out for itself. Soup was boiling in a large cauldron, and hares and rabbits were roasting on the spit.

'You shall sleep with me and all my little animals tonight,' said the robber-girl, after they had had something to eat and drink. So she took Gerda to a corner of the hall, where some straw and carpets were laid down. Above them, on perches, were more than a hundred pigeons, who all seemed to be asleep, although they moved slightly when the two little girls came near them. 'These all belong to me,' said the robber-girl; and she seized the nearest to her, held it by the feet and shook it till it flapped its wings. 'Kiss it,' she cried, flapping it in Gerda's face. 'There sit the wood pigeons,' continued she, pointing to a number of laths and a cage which had been fixed into the walls, near one of the openings. 'Both rascals would fly away directly, if they were not closely locked up. And here is my old sweetheart "Ba"; and she dragged out a reindeer by the horn; he wore a bright copper ring round his neck, and was tied up. 'We are obliged to hold him tight too, or else he would run away from us also. I tickle his neck every evening with my sharp knife, which frightens him very much.' And then the robber-girl drew a long knife from a chink in the wall, and let it slide gently over the reindeer's neck. The poor animal began to kick, and the little robber-girl laughed, and pulled down Gerda into bed with her.

'Will you have that knife with you while you are asleep?' asked Gerda, looking at it in great fright.

'I always sleep with the knife by me,' said the robber-girl. 'No one knows what may happen. But now tell me again all about little Kay, and why you went out into the world.'

So Gerda repeated her story over again, while the wood pigeons in the cage over her cooed, and the other pigeons slept. The little robber-girl put one arm across Gerda's neck, and held the knife in the other, and was soon fast asleep and snoring. But Gerda could not close her eyes at all; she knew not whether she was to live or die. The robbers sat around the fire, singing and drinking, and the old woman stumbled about. It was a terrible sight for a little girl to witness.

Then the wood pigeons said, 'Coo, coo; we have seen little Kay. A white fowl carried his sledge, and he sat in the carriage of the Snow Queen, which drove through the wood while we were lying in our nest.

She blew upon us, and all the young ones died excepting us two. Coo, coo.'

'What are you saying up there?' cried Gerda. 'Where was the Snow Queen going?'

'She was most likely travelling to Lapland, where there is always snow and ice. Ask the reindeer that is fastened up there with a rope.'

'Yes, there is always snow and ice,' said the reindeer; 'and it is a glorious place; you can leap and run about freely on the sparkling ice plains. The Snow Queen has her summer tent there, but her strong castle is at the North Pole, on an island called Spitzbergen.'

'Oh, Kay, little Kay!' sighed Gerda.

'Lie still,' said the robber-girl, 'or I shall run my knife into your body.'

In the morning Gerda told her all that the wood pigeons had said; and the little robber-girl looked quite serious, and nodded her head, and said, 'That is all talk, that is all talk. Do you know where Lapland is?' she asked the reindeer.

'Who should know better than I do?' said the animal, while his eyes sparkled. 'I was born and brought up there, and used to run about the snow-covered plains.'

'Now listen,' said the robber-girl; 'all our men are going out now, but my mother is here, and will stay behind; but at noon she always drinks out of a great bottle, and after that she'll sleep. Then I'll do something for you.' Then she jumped out of bed, clasped her mother round the neck and pulled her by the beard, crying, 'My own little nanny goat, good morning.' Then her mother filliped her nose till it was quite red; yet she did it all for love.

When the mother had drunk out of the bottle and was gone to sleep, the little robber-maiden went to the reindeer and said, 'I should like very much to tickle your neck a few times more with my knife, for it makes you look so funny; but never mind – I will untie your cord, and set you free, so that you may run away to Lapland; but you must make good use of your legs and carry this little girl to the castle of the Snow Queen, where her friend is. You have heard what she told me, for she spoke loud enough, and you were listening.'

Then the reindeer jumped for joy; and the little robber-girl lifted Gerda on his back, and tied her on firmly and gave her her own little cushion to sit on.

'Here are your fur boots for you,' said she, 'for it will be very cold; but I must keep the muff; it is so pretty. However, you shall not be frozen for the want of it; here are my mother's large warm mittens; they will reach up to your elbows. Let me put them on. There, now your hands look just like my mother's.'

Gerda wept for joy.

'I don't like to see you crying,' said the little robber-girl; 'you ought to look happy now. See, here are two loaves and a ham, so that you need not starve.' These were fastened on the reindeer, and then the little robber-maiden opened the door, coaxed in all the great dogs, and then cut the string with which the reindeer was fastened, with her sharp knife, and said, 'Now run, but mind you take good care of the little girl.' And then Gerda stretched out her hand, with the great mitten on it, towards the little robber-girl, and said, 'Farewell,' and away flew the reindeer, over stumps and stones, through the great forest, over marshes and plains, as quickly as he could. The wolves howled, and the ravens screamed; while up in the sky quivered red lights like flames of fire. 'There are my old northern lights,' said the reindeer; 'see how they flash.' And he ran on, day and night, still faster and faster. They ate the loaves and the ham and then at last they reached Lapland.

The Lapland Woman and the Finland Woman

They stopped at a little hut. It was very mean-looking. The roof sloped nearly down to the ground, and the door was so low that the family had to creep in on their hands and knees when they went in and out. There was no one at home except an old Lapland woman, who was cooking fish by the light of an oil lamp. The reindeer told her all about Gerda's story, after having first told his own, which seemed to him the most important. Poor Gerda was so pinched with the cold that she could not speak. 'Oh, you poor things,' said the Lapland woman, 'you still have a long way to go. You must travel more than a hundred miles further, to Finland. The Snow Queen lives there now, and she burns blue lights every evening. I will write a few words on a dried fish, for I have no paper, and you can take it from me to the Finland woman who lives there; she can give you better information than I can.'

So when Gerda was warmed, and had taken something to eat and drink, the woman wrote a few words on the dried fish and told Gerda to take great care of it. Then she tied her again on the reindeer, and he set off at full speed.

Flash, flash, went the beautiful blue northern lights in the air the whole night long. And at length they reached Finland, and knocked at the chimney of the Finland woman's hut, for it had no door above the ground. They crept in, but it was so terribly hot inside that that woman wore scarcely any clothes; she was small and very dirty-looking. She loosened little Gerda's dress, and took off the fur boots and the mittens, or Gerda would have been unable to bear the heat; and then she placed a piece of ice on the reindeer's head, and read what was written on the dried fish. After she had read it three times she knew it by heart, so she popped the fish into the soup saucepan, as she knew it was good to eat and she never wasted anything.

The reindeer told his own story first, and then little Gerda's, and the Finlander twinkled with her clever eyes, but she said nothing. 'You are so clever,' said the reindeer. 'Can't you give this little girl something which will make her as strong as twelve men, to overcome the Snow Queen?'

'The power of twelve men!' said the Finland woman. 'That would be of very little use.' But she went to a shelf and took down and unrolled a large skin, on which were inscribed wonderful characters, and she read till the perspiration ran down from her forehead. At last her eyes began to twinkle again; so she drew the reindeer into a corner, and whispered to him while she laid a fresh piece of ice on his head. 'Little Kay is really with the Snow Queen, but he finds everything there so much to his taste and his liking that he believes it is the finest place in the world; but this is because he has a piece of broken glass in his heart, and a little piece of glass in his eye. These must be taken out, or he will never be a human being again and the Snow Queen will retain her power over him.'

'But can you not give little Gerda something to help her to conquer this power?'

'I can give her no greater power than she has already,' said the woman; 'don't you see how strong that is? How men and animals are obliged to serve her, and how well she has got through the world, barefooted as she is. She cannot receive any power from me greater than she now has, which consists in her own purity and innocence of heart. If she cannot herself obtain access to the Snow Queen, and remove the glass fragments from little Kay, we can do nothing to help her. Two miles from here the Snow Queen's garden begins; you can carry the little girl so far, and set her down by the large bush which stands in the snow, covered with red berries. Do not stay gossiping, but come back here as quickly as you can.' Then the Finland woman lifted little Gerda upon the reindeer, and he ran away with her as quickly as he could.

'Oh, I have forgotten my boots and my mittens,' cried little Gerda as soon as she felt the cutting cold, but the reindeer dared not stop, so he ran on till he reached the bush with the red berries; here he set Gerda down, and he kissed her, and the great bright tears trickled over the animal's cheeks; then he left her and ran back as fast as he could.

There stood poor Gerda, without shoes, without gloves, in the midst of cold, dreary, ice-bound Finland. She ran forward as quickly as she could, when a whole regiment of snowflakes came round her; they did not, however, fall from the sky, which was quite clear and glittering with the northern lights. The snowflakes ran along the ground, and the nearer they came to her, the larger they appeared. Gerda remembered how large and beautiful they looked through the burning glass. But these were really larger, and much more terrible, for they were alive, and were the guards of the Snow Queen, and had the strangest shapes. Some were like great porcupines, others like twisted serpents with their heads stretching out, and some few were like little fat bears with their hair bristled; but all were dazzlingly white, and all were living snowflakes.

Then little Gerda repeated the Lord's Prayer, and the cold was so great that she could see her own breath come out of her mouth like steam as she uttered the words. The steam appeared to increase, as she continued her prayer, till it took the shape of little angels who grew larger the moment they touched the earth. They all wore helmets on their heads, and carried spears and shields. Their number continued to increase more and more; and by the time Gerda had finished her prayers, a whole legion stood round her. They thrust their spears into the terrible snowflakes, so that they shivered into a hundred pieces, and little Gerda could go forward with courage and safety. The angels stroked her hands and feet, so that she felt the cold less, and she hastened on to the Snow Queen's castle.

But now we must see what Kay is doing. In truth he was not thinking of little Gerda, and never supposed she could be standing in the front of the palace.

The Palace of the Snow Queen

The walls of the palace were formed of drifted snow, and the windows and doors of the cutting winds. There were more than a hundred rooms in it, all as if they had been formed with snow blown together. The largest of them extended for several miles; they were all lighted up by the vivid northern lights, and they were so large and empty, so icy cold and glittering! In the midst of its empty, endless hall of snow was a frozen lake, broken on its surface into a thousand pieces. These pieces were so exactly alike that it might well be thought a work of more than human skill. In the centre of this lake sat the Snow Queen, when she was at home. She called the lake 'The Mirror of Reason', and said that it was the best, and indeed the only one in the world.

Little Kay was quite blue with cold, indeed almost black, but he did not feel it, for the Snow Queen had kissed away the icy shiverings, and his heart was already a lump of ice. He dragged some sharp, flat pieces of ice to and fro, and placed them together in all kinds of positions, as if he wished to make something out of them; just as people do with a Chinese puzzle. Kay could make the most curious and complete figures – and in his eyes these were very important. But this opinion was owing to the piece of glass still sticking in his eye. He composed many complete figures, forming different words, but there was one word

he never could manage to form, although he wished it very much. It was the word 'Eternity'. The Snow Queen had said to him, 'When you can find out this, you shall be your own master, and I will give you the whole world and a new pair of skates.' But he could never do it.

'Now I must hasten away to warmer countries,' said the Snow Queen. 'I will go and look into the black craters of the tops of the burning mountains (she meant the volcanoes Etna and Vesuvius) and I shall make them look white. And away flew the Snow Queen, leaving little Kay quite alone in the great hall which was so many miles in length; so he sat and looked at his pieces of ice, and was thinking so deeply, and sat so still, that anyone might have supposed he was frozen.

Just at this moment little Gerda came through the great door of the castle. Cutting winds were raging around her, but she offered up a prayer and the winds sank down as if they were going to sleep; and she went on till she came to the large empty hall and caught sight of Kay. She knew him immediately and flew to him and threw her arms round his neck. She held him fast, crying, 'Kay, dear little Kay, I have found you at last.'

But he sat quite still, stiff and cold.

Then little Gerda wept hot tears, which fell on his breast, and penetrated into his heart, and thawed the lump of ice, and washed away the little piece of glass which had stuck there. Then he looked at her, and she sang:

'Roses bloom and cease to be,
But we shall the Christ-child see.'

Then Kay burst into tears, and he wept so that the splinter of glass swam out of his eye. Then he recognised Gerda and said joyfully, 'Gerda, dear little Gerda, where have you been all this time, and where have I been?'

And he looked all around him, and said, 'How cold it is, and how large and empty it all looks,' and he clung to Gerda, and she laughed and wept for joy. It was so pleasing to see them that the pieces of ice even danced about; and when they were tired and went to lie down, they formed themselves into the letters of the word which the Snow Queen had said he must find out before he could be his own master and have the whole world and a pair of new skates. Then Gerda kissed his cheeks, and they became blooming; and she kissed his eyes, and they shone like her own; she kissed his hands and his feet, and then he became quite healthy and cheerful. The Snow Queen might come home now when she pleased, for there stood his certainty of freedom, in the word she wanted, written in shining letters of ice.

Then they took each other by the hand and left the great palace of ice. As they walked the winds were at rest, and the sun burst forth. When they arrived at the bush with red berries, there stood the reindeer waiting for them, and he had brought another young reindeer with him, whose udders were full, and the children drank her warm milk.

Then they carried Kay and Gerda first to the Finland woman, where they warmed themselves thoroughly in the hot room, and she gave them directions about their journey home. Next they went to the Lapland woman, who had made some new clothes for them, and put their sleighs in order. Both the reindeer ran by their side, and followed them as far as the boundaries of the country, where the first green leaves were budding. And here they took leave of the two reindeer and the Lapland woman, and all said, 'Farewell.' Then the birds began to twitter, and the forest too was full of green young leaves; and out of it came a beautiful horse, which Gerda remembered, for it was one which had drawn the golden coach. A young girl was riding upon it, with a shining red cap on her head, and pistols in her belt. It was the little robber-maiden, who had got tired of staying at home; she was going first to the north, and if that did not suit her, she meant to try some other part of the world. She recognised Gerda immediately, and Gerda remembered her: it was a joyful meeting.

'You are a fine fellow to go gadding about in this way,' said she to little Kay. 'I should like to know whether you deserve that anyone should go to the end of the world to find you.'

But Gerda patted her cheeks, and asked after the prince and princess.

'They are gone to foreign countries,' said the robber-girl.

'And the crow?' asked Gerda.

'Oh, the crow is dead,' she replied; 'his tame sweetheart is now a widow and wears a bit of black cloth round her leg. She mourns very pitifully and chatters more than ever. But now tell me how you managed to get your friend back.'

Then Gerda and Kay told her all about it.

'Snip, snap, snare! It's all right at last,' said the robber-girl.

Then she took both their hands, and promised that if ever she should pass through the town, she would call and pay them a visit. And then she rode away into the wide world. Gerda and Kay went hand in hand towards home. And wherever they went it was spring, beautiful spring, with its flowers and green leaves. Very soon they recognised the large town where they lived, and the tall steeples of the churches, in which the sweet bells were ringing a merry peal as they entered it and found their way to their grandmother's door. They went upstairs into the little room, where all looked just as it used to do. The old clock was going 'tick, tick', and the hands pointed to the time of day, but as they passed through the door into the room they perceived that they were both grown up, and become a man and woman. The roses out on the roof were in full bloom, and peeped in at the window; and there stood the little chairs, on which they had sat when children; and Kay and Gerda seated themselves each on their own chair and held each other by the hand, while the cold empty grandeur of the Snow Queen's palace vanished from their memories like a painful dream. The grandmother sat in God's bright sunshine, and she read aloud from the Bible, 'Except ye become as little children, ye shall in no wise enter into the kingdom of God.' And Kay and Gerda looked into each other's eyes, and all at once understood the words of the old song,

> *'Roses bloom and cease to be,*
> *But we shall the Christ-child see.'*

And there they both sat, grown up, yet children at heart; and it was summer – warm, beautiful summer.

NIGHT

12

The Twelve Days of Christmas

Traditional

On the first day of Christmas my true love sent to me: a partridge in a pear tree.

On the second day of Christmas my true love sent to me: two turtledoves and a partridge in a pear tree.

On the third day of Christmas my true love sent to me: three French hens, two turtledoves and a partridge in a pear tree.

On the fourth day of Christmas my true love sent to me: four calling birds, three French hens, two turtledoves and a partridge in a pear tree.

On the fifth day of Christmas my true love sent to me:
five golden rings. Four calling birds, three French hens, two
turtledoves and a partridge in a pear tree.

On the sixth day of Christmas my true love sent to me:
Six geese a-laying, five golden rings. Four calling birds, three
French hens, two turtledoves and a partridge in a pear tree.

On the seventh day of Christmas my true love sent to me:
seven swans a-swimming, six geese a-laying, five golden rings.
Four calling birds, three French hens, two turtledoves and a
partridge in a pear tree.

On the eighth day of Christmas my true love sent to me:
eight maids a-milking, seven swans a-swimming, six geese
a-laying, five golden rings. Four calling birds, three French hens,
two turtledoves and a partridge in a pear tree.

On the ninth day of Christmas my true love sent to me:
nine ladies dancing, eight maids a-milking, seven swans
a-swimming, six geese a-laying, five golden rings. Four calling
birds, three French hens, two turtledoves and a partridge in a
pear tree.

On the tenth day of Christmas my true love sent to me:
ten lords a-leaping, nine ladies dancing, eight maids a-milking, seven
swans a-swimming, six geese a-laying, five golden rings. Four calling
birds, three French hens, two turtledoves and a partridge in a pear tree.

On the eleventh day of Christmas my true love sent to me:
eleven pipers piping, ten lords a-leaping, nine ladies dancing, eight maids
a-milking, seven swans a-swimming, six geese a-laying, five golden rings.
Four calling birds, three French hens, two turtledoves and a partridge in
a pear tree.

On the twelfth day of Christmas my true love sent to me: twelve drummers drumming, eleven pipers piping, ten lords a-leaping, nine ladies dancing, eight maids a-milking, seven swans a-swimming, six geese a-laying, five golden rings. Four calling birds, three French hens, two turtledoves and a partridge in a pear tree.

NIGHT

13

Old Fezziwig's Party

An extract from *A Christmas Carol*

By Charles Dickens

Old Fezziwig's Party

An extract from *A Christmas Carol*
By Charles Dickens

Old Fezziwig laid down his pen, and looked up at the clock, which pointed to the hour of seven. He rubbed his hands; adjusted his capacious waistcoat; laughed all over himself, from his shoes to his organ of benevolence; and called out in a comfortable, oily, rich, fat, jovial voice: 'Yo ho, there! Ebenezer! Dick! Yo ho, my boys!' said Fezziwig. 'No more work tonight. Christmas Eve, Dick. Christmas, Ebenezer. Let's have the shutters up,' cried old Fezziwig, with a sharp clap of his hands, 'before a man can say Jack Robinson.'

You wouldn't believe how those two fellows went at it. They charged into the street with the shutters – one, two, three – had them up in their places – four, five, six – barred them and pinned then – seven, eight, nine – and came back before you could have got to twelve, panting like racehorses.

'Hilli-ho!' cried old Fezziwig, skipping down from the high desk, with wonderful agility. 'Clear away, my lads, and let's have lots of room here. Hilli-ho, Dick! Chirrup, Ebenezer.'

Clear away! There was nothing they wouldn't have cleared away, or couldn't have cleared away, with old Fezziwig looking on. It was done in a minute. Every movable was packed off, as if it were dismissed from public life for evermore; the floor was swept and watered, the lamps were trimmed, fuel was heaped upon the fire; and the warehouse was as snug, and warm, and dry, and bright a ballroom as you would desire to see upon a winter's night.

In came a fiddler with a music book, and went up to the lofty desk, and made an orchestra of it, and tuned like fifty stomach aches. In came Mrs Fezziwig, one vast substantial smile. In came the three Miss Fezziwigs, beaming and lovable. In came the six young followers whose hearts they broke. In came all the young men and women employed in the business. In came the housemaid, with her cousin, the baker. In came the cook, with her brother's particular friend, the milkman. In came the boy from over the way, who was suspected of not having board enough from his master; trying to hide himself behind the girl from next door but one, who was proved to have had her ears pulled by her mistress. In they all came, one after another; some shyly, some boldly, some gracefully, some awkwardly, some pushing, some pulling; in they all came, anyhow and everyhow. Away they all went, twenty couple at once; hands half round and back again the other way; down the middle and up again; round and round in various stages of affectionate grouping; old top couple always turning up in the wrong place; new top couple starting off again, as soon as they got there; all top couples at last, and not a bottom one to help them. When this result was brought about, old Fezziwig, clapping his hands to stop the dance, cried out, 'Well done!' and the fiddler plunged his hot face into a pot of porter, especially provided for that purpose. But scorning rest, upon his reappearance, he instantly began again, though there were no dancers yet, as if the other fiddler had been carried home, exhausted, on a shutter, and he were a brand-new man resolved to beat him out of sight, or perish.

There were more dances, and there were forfeits, and more dances, and there was cake, and there was negus, and there was a great piece of Cold Roast, and there was a great piece of Cold Boiled, and there were mince pies, and plenty of beer. But the great effect of the evening came after the Roast and Boiled, when the fiddler (an artful dog, mind! The sort of man who knew his business better than you or I could have told it him!) struck up 'Sir Roger de Coverley'. Then old Fezziwig stood out to dance with Mrs Fezziwig. Top couple too; with a good stiff piece of work cut out for them; three or four and twenty pair of partners; people who were not to be trifled with; people who would dance, and had no notion of walking.

But if they had been twice as many – ah, four times – old Fezziwig would have been a match for them, and so would Mrs Fezziwig. As to her, she was worthy to be his partner in every sense of the term. If that's not high praise, tell me higher, and I'll use it. A positive light appeared to issue from Fezziwig's calves. They shone in every part of the dance like moons. You couldn't have predicted, at any given time, what would have become of them next. And when old Fezziwig and Mrs Fezziwig had gone all through the dance; advance and retire, both hands to your partner, bow and curtsy, corkscrew, thread-the-needle, and back again to your place; Fezziwig cut – cut so deftly, that he appeared to wink with his legs, and came upon his feet again without a stagger.

When the clock struck eleven, this domestic ball broke up. Mr and Mrs Fezziwig took their stations, one on either side of the door, and shaking hands with every person individually as he or she went out, wished him or her a merry Christmas. When everybody had retired but the two prentices, they did the same to them; and thus the cheerful voices died away, and the lads were left to their beds, which were under a counter in the back shop.

NIGHT

14

Professor Branestawm's Christmas Tree

By Norman Hunter

Professor Branestawm's Christmas Tree

By Norman Hunter

Professor Branestawm's fantastic inventions are always getting him and his good friend Colonel Dedshott into all manner of trouble.

There had never been a Christmas party at Professor Branestawm's house before. Because the Professor was always so immersed in thinking about new inventions he never had time left to think of old customs. But this time the Professor was absolutely going to have a Christmas party, because he had invented a present-giving invention.

'I have always thought, Dedshott,' said the Professor to the Colonel, 'that the, er, traditional Christmas tree offered possibilities for, um, development,' by which of course he meant it could be interestingly fiddled about with.

The Professor swung his new invention round and the Colonel got a daisy one on the ear from a sticking-out part of the machinery.

'My idea,' said the Professor, 'consists of a purely automatic Christmas tree, fitted with a mechanical present distributor coupled to a greetings-speaking device and a gift-wrapping attachment so that the, er, recipients receive their gifts suitably, um ah, wrapped up and accompanied by a Christmas greeting.'

He pulled a lever, pressed some buttons and twiddled a twiddler.

Pop whizzetty chug chug. 'Good King Wenceslas,' sang the machine. 'Look out!' cried the Professor. A highly decorative parcel shot out of the tree and landed on the Colonel's lap accompanied by a hearty 'Happy Christmas!' from the tree and 'By Jove, what!' from the Colonel.

'Jolly clever, my word,' he grunted. 'How does it work, eh?'

The moment he asked the question the Colonel wished he hadn't. He knew what would happen. The Professor would erupt in complicated explainings that would make his head go round and round. But this time it was all right. The Professor didn't explain anything. He came over all coy and said, 'Wait until my Christmas party, Dedshott.'

The Professor's party started off all nice and ordinary, apart from the fact that it took place in November because the Professor couldn't wait to show off his invention. The guests arrived with presents for the Professor.

Mrs Flittersnoop gave him a sweet little rack with five hooks for his five pairs of spectacles, which was meant for keys, but anyway the Professor hung his coat on it and collapsed the whole thing.

Colonel Dedshott weighed in with a paperweight made to look like a small cannon, which made you feel you had to wait for it to go off though it never did.

The Mayor presented a photo of Pagwell High Street, in which he had a shop, in a green plush frame with gilt corners.

The Vicar handed the Professor a tastefully bound volume of his own sermons, autographed in mauve ink with ecclesiastical squiggles.

Sister Aggie's little girl was given a packet of toffee to give the Professor but she ate it on the way and gave him instead a sticky kiss on the forehead, which helped to keep his spectacles on. The postman brought a collection of used stamps with something wrong with them which made them much more valuable than they ought to have been.

'Er, ah, thank you,' said the Professor. 'Now come this way, please.' He led the way down the passage, into the kitchen by mistake and nearly into the gas cooker and eventually after much pushing and excuse-me's they all got packed into his study where the automatic mechanical Christmas tree stood.

'Here is the present distributor,' said the Professor, pointing to a row of eager-looking levers. 'They are labelled with your names. All you have to, ah, do, is pull the lever with your name on.'

'Marvellous!' cried the Colonel.

'Shall I declare the tree open?' said the Mayor and the Vicar, both at once. Then without waiting for an answer they both coughed and, in very high-class voices, said, 'I have pleasuah in declaring the tree open, hrrrmph.'

Soon levers were being pulled, the machine was clanking away, the air was full of Christmas music and hearty greetings and the crash of paper parcels being excitably unwrapped.

The Mayor got a pair of silk stockings and a bottle of lavender water, which were really intended for Mrs Flittersnoop, because the Professor had got the names on the levers muddled up.

'Now that's what I call real kind,' cried Mrs Flittersnoop. Then she said 'Oh!' in a rather pale voice when she found she had got a packet of corn cure and a tin of tobacco shaped like a pillar box, which should have gone to the postman.

Sister Aggie found herself with a box of cigars. The Vicar had a china doll with no clothes on. Colonel Dedshott's present was a yellow bonnet with imitation cherries on it. The Pagwell Library man got a packet of large square dog biscuits and wondered if they were a new kind of book.

'I fear there has been some mistake,' murmured the Vicar. 'May I be permitted to exchange this charming gift for something more suitable?' He pushed the china doll into the machine and pulled one of the levers. At the same time the Mayor and sister Aggie pushed their presents back and started pressing not-meant-to-be-pressed buttons, to change their presents.

'No, no, no!' cried the Professor, clashing his spectacles.

But he was too late. The automatic Christmas tree evidently resented having its presents returned. It rang out a burst of Christmas bells that sounded like a fire engine, emitted a cloud of dirty green smoke, shouted, 'Merry Christmas on the feast of Stephen!' and shot out of the house and down the road.

'After it!' roared the Colonel, who reckoned he knew how to deal with the situation.

They all tore after the machine that was shouting a mixed version of 'The Twelve Days of Christmas'. Colonel Dedshott drew his sword and rushed at it. The machine took it away and returned it gift-wrapped.

'Five golden things,' sang the machine, careering down the road, giving out presents and Christmas wishes right and left. Three little boys with a November the fifth Guy who were asking for pennies got instead a parcel of files and screwdrivers that were the Professor's Christmas present for himself. A lady coming out of a supermarket was presented with the Vicar's china doll and a yard and a half of 'The Holly and the Ivy' sung out of tune.

'Dash round the other way and cut it off,' shouted the Colonel to the driver of a steam roller. But steam rollers are absolutely no good at dashing.

The Professor flew past on his bicycle in hot pursuit, but the machine scattered a box of coloured marbles on the road and he side-slipped into the Mayor's arms.

'Thirty-five maids a-dancing, ninety ladies singing, no end of a lot of swans splashing about, five golden rings,' sang the machine. It tore down Uppington Street, round the Square, turned left into Wright Street, hotly pursued by the Professor, his guests and crowds of Pagwell people who were shouting, 'Stop, thief!' which was all they could think of to shout.

The machine ran out of presents and started picking up anything it could see and wrapping it in anything handy. A policeman held up his hand to make it stop and was given a piece of paving stone wrapped in an advertisement for second-hand bicycles.

On rushed the machine, across the High Street, smack into the smash-and-grab robber who was just dashing out of the jeweller's shop with a sack full of valuables.

'And a partridge up a gum tree,' shouted the machine. It sat on the robber, tore open the sack and was only just stopped from handing out watches and pearl necklaces all around by the arrival of an absolute heap of policemen. They arrested the robber and would have arrested the machine too, only Professor Branestawm arrived just in time to turn off the works and explain what had happened, which the policemen didn't believe anyway.

'Disturbing the peace, y'know,' said a police sergeant with three chins. 'Conduct likely to cause. . .'

But the Professor and the Colonel between them had got the Christmas tree apart, packed it into a passing wheelbarrow, given a new fifty-pence piece to the man who was pushing it and persuaded him to take it back to the Professor's house.

And everything turned out nicely because the jeweller gave the Professor a reward for catching the robber, so the Professor was able to buy some very handsome presents to give to everyone at Christmas, which he did by the very unoriginal but completely satisfactory way of handing them over and saying, 'Happy um – ah – Christmas.'

NIGHT

15

In the Bleak Midwinter

By Christina Rossetti

In the Bleak Midwinter

By Christina Rossetti

In the bleak midwinter, frosty wind made moan,
Earth stood hard as iron, water like a stone;
Snow had fallen, snow on snow, snow on snow,
In the bleak midwinter, long ago.

Our God, Heaven cannot hold Him, nor earth sustain;
Heaven and earth shall flee away when He comes to reign.
In the bleak midwinter a stable place sufficed
The Lord God Almighty, Jesus Christ.

Enough for Him, whom cherubim worship night and day,
Breastful of milk, and a mangerful of hay;
Enough for Him, whom angels fall before,
The ox and ass and camel which adore.

Angels and archangels may have gathered there,
Cherubim and seraphim thronged the air;
But His mother only, in her maiden bliss,
Worshipped the beloved with a kiss.

What can I give Him, poor as I am?
If I were a shepherd, I would bring a lamb;
If I were a Wise Man, I would do my part;
Yet what I can I give Him: give my heart.

NIGHT

16

The Selfish Giant

By Oscar Wilde

The Selfish Giant

By Oscar Wilde

Every afternoon, as they were coming from school, the children used to go and play in the Giant's garden.

It was a large lovely garden, with soft green grass. Here and there over the grass stood beautiful flowers like stars, and there were twelve peach trees that in the springtime broke out into delicate blossoms of pink and pearl, and in the autumn bore rich fruit. The birds sat on the trees and sang so sweetly that the children used to stop their games in order to listen to them. 'How happy we are here!' they cried to each other.

One day the Giant came back. He had been to visit his friend the Cornish ogre, and had stayed with him for seven years. After the seven years were over he had said all that he had to say, for his conversation was limited, and he determined to return to his own castle. When he arrived he saw the children playing in the garden.

'What are you doing here?' he cried in a very gruff voice, and the children ran away.

'My own garden is my own garden,' said the Giant; 'anyone can understand that, and I will allow nobody to play in it but myself.' So he built a high wall all round it, and put up a noticeboard.

TRESPASSERS WILL BE PROSECUTED

He was a very selfish giant.

The poor children had now nowhere to play. They tried to play on the road, but the road was very dusty and full of hard stones, and they did not like it. They used to wander round the high wall when their lessons were over, and talk about the beautiful garden inside.

'How happy we were there,' they said to each other.

Then the Spring came, and all over the country there were little blossoms and little birds. Only in the garden of the Selfish Giant it was still Winter. The birds did not care to sing in it as there were no children, and the trees forgot to blossom. Once a beautiful flower put its head out from the grass, but when it saw the noticeboard it was so sorry for the children that it slipped back into the ground again and went off to sleep.

The only people who were pleased were the Snow and the Frost. 'Spring has forgotten this garden,' they cried, 'so we will live here all the year round.' The Snow covered up the grass with her great white cloak, and the Frost painted all the trees silver.

Then they invited the North Wind to stay with them, and he came. He was wrapped in furs, and he roared all day about the garden, and blew the chimneypots down. 'This is a delightful spot,' he said. 'We must ask the Hail on a visit.'

So the Hail came. Every day for three hours he rattled on the roof of the castle till he broke most of the slates, and then he ran round and round the garden as fast as he could go. He was dressed in grey, and his breath was like ice.

'I cannot understand why the Spring is so late in coming,' said the Selfish Giant, as he sat at the window and looked out at his cold white garden; 'I hope there will be a change in the weather.'

But the Spring never came, nor the Summer. The Autumn gave golden fruit to every garden, but to the Giant's garden she gave none. 'He is too selfish,' she said. So it was always Winter there, and the North Wind, and the Hail, and the Frost, and the Snow danced about through the trees.

One morning the Giant was lying awake in bed when he heard some lovely music. It sounded so sweet to his ears that he thought it must be the king's musicians passing by. It was really only a little linnet singing outside his window, but it was so long since he had heard a bird sing in his garden that it seemed to him to be the most beautiful music in the world. Then the Hail stopped dancing over his head, and the North Wind ceased roaring, and a delicious perfume came to him through the open casement. 'I believe the Spring has come at last,' said the Giant; and he jumped out of bed and looked out.

What did he see?

He saw a most wonderful sight. Through a little hole in the wall the children had crept in, and they were sitting in the branches of the trees. In every tree that he could see there was a little child. And the trees were so glad to have the children back again that they had covered themselves with blossoms, and were waving their arms gently above the children's heads. The birds were flying about and twittering with delight, and the flowers were looking up through the green grass and laughing. It was a lovely scene, only in one corner it was still Winter. It was the furthest corner of the garden, and in it was standing a little boy. He was so small that he could not reach up to the branches of the tree, and he was wandering all round it, crying bitterly. The poor tree was still quite covered with frost and snow, and the North Wind was blowing and roaring above it. 'Climb up, little boy!' said the tree, and it bent its branches down as low as it could; but the little boy was too tiny.

And the Giant's heart melted as he looked out. 'How selfish I have been!' he said; 'now I know why the Spring would not come here. I will put that poor little boy on the top of the tree, and then I will knock down the wall, and my garden shall be the children's playground for ever and ever.' He was really very sorry for what he had done.

So he crept downstairs and opened the front door quite softly, and went out into the garden. But when the children saw him they were so frightened that they all ran away, and the garden became Winter again. Only the little boy did not run, for his eyes were so full of tears that he did not see the Giant coming. And the Giant stole up behind him and took him gently in his hand, and put him up into the tree.

And the tree broke at once into blossom, and the birds came and sang on it, and the little boy stretched out his two arms and flung them round the Giant's neck and kissed him. And the other children, when they saw that the Giant was not wicked any longer, came running back, and with them came the Spring. 'It is your garden now, little children,' said the Giant, and he took a great axe and knocked down the wall. And when the people were going to market at twelve o'clock they found the Giant playing with the children in the most beautiful garden they had ever seen.

All day long they played, and in the evening they came to the Giant to bid him goodbye.

'But where is your little companion?' he said. 'The boy I put into the tree.' The Giant loved him the best because he had kissed him.

'We don't know,' answered the children. 'He has gone away.'

'You must tell him to be sure and come here tomorrow,' said the Giant. But the children said that they did not know where he lived, and had never seen him before; and the Giant felt very sad.

Every afternoon, when school was over, the children came and played with the Giant. But the little boy whom the Giant loved was never seen again. The Giant was very kind to all the children, yet he longed for his first little friend, and often spoke of him. 'How I would like to see him!' he used to say.

Years went over, and the Giant grew very old and feeble. He could not play about any more, so he sat in a huge armchair, and watched the children at their games and admired his garden. 'I have many beautiful flowers,' he said, 'but the children are the most beautiful flowers of all.'

One winter morning he looked out of his window as he was dressing. He did not hate the Winter now, for he knew that it was merely the Spring asleep, and that the flowers were resting.

Suddenly he rubbed his eyes in wonder, and looked and looked. It certainly was a marvellous sight. In the furthest corner of the garden was a tree quite covered with lovely white blossoms. Its branches were all golden, and silver fruit hung down from them, and underneath it stood the little boy he had loved.

Downstairs ran the Giant in great joy, and out into the garden. He hastened across the grass and came near to the child. And when he came quite close his face grew red with anger, and he said, 'Who hath dared to wound thee?' For on the palms of the child's hands were the prints of two nails, and the prints of two nails were on the little feet.

'Who hath dared to wound thee?' cried the Giant; 'tell me, that I may take my big sword and slay him.'

'Nay!' answered the child; 'but these are the wounds of Love.'

'Who art thou?' said the Giant, and a strange awe fell on him, and he knelt before the little child.

And the child smiled on the Giant, and said to him, 'You let me play once in your garden; today you shall come with me to my garden, which is Paradise.'

And when the children ran in that afternoon, they found the Giant lying dead under the tree, all covered with white blossoms.

NIGHT

17

An extract from

Little Women

By Louisa May Alcott

An extract from

Little Women

By Louisa May Alcott

'Christmas won't be Christmas without any presents,' grumbled Jo, lying on the rug.

'It's so dreadful to be poor!' sighed Meg, looking down at her old dress.

'I don't think it's fair for some girls to have plenty of pretty things, and other girls nothing at all,' added little Amy, with an injured sniff.

'We've got Father and Mother, and each other,' said Beth contentedly from her corner.

The four young faces on which the firelight shone brightened at the cheerful words, but darkened again as Jo said sadly, 'We haven't got Father, and shall not have him for a long time.' She didn't say 'perhaps never', but each silently added it, thinking of Father far away, where the fighting was.

Nobody spoke for a minute; then Meg said in an altered tone, 'You know the reason Mother proposed not having any presents this Christmas was because it is going to be a hard winter for everyone; and she thinks we ought not to spend money for pleasure, when our men are suffering so in the army. We can't do much, but we can make our little sacrifices, and ought to do it gladly. But I am afraid I don't.' And Meg shook her head, as she thought regretfully of all the pretty things she wanted.

'But I don't think the little we should spend would do any good. We've each got a dollar, and the army wouldn't be much helped by our giving that. I agree not to expect anything from Mother or you, but I do want to buy *Undine and Sintram* for myself. I've wanted it so long,' said Jo, who was a bookworm.

'I planned to spend mine on new music,' said Beth, with a little sigh, which no one heard but the hearth brush and kettle holder.

'I shall get a nice box of Faber's drawing pencils. I really need them,' said Amy decidedly.

'Mother didn't say anything about our money, and she won't wish us to give up everything. Let's each buy what we want, and have a little fun. I'm sure we work hard enough to earn it,' cried Jo, examining the heels of her shoes in a gentlemanly manner.

'I know I do, teaching those tiresome children nearly all day, when I'm longing to enjoy myself at home,' began Meg, in the complaining tone again.

'You don't have half such a hard time as I do,' said Jo. 'How would you like to be shut up for hours with a nervous, fussy old lady, who keeps you trotting, is never satisfied and worries you till you you're ready to fly out the window or cry?'

'It's naughty to fret, but I do think washing dishes and keeping things tidy is the worst work in the world. It makes me cross, and my hands get so stiff I can't practise well at all.' And Beth looked at her rough hands with a sigh that anyone could hear that time.

'I don't believe any of you suffer as I do,' cried Amy, 'for you don't have to go to school with impertinent girls, who plague you if you don't know your lessons, and laugh at your dresses, and label your father if he isn't rich, and insult you when your nose isn't nice.'

'If you mean libel, I'd say so, and not talk about labels, as if Papa was a pickle bottle,' advised Jo, laughing.

'I know what I mean, and you needn't be statirical about it. It's proper to use good words, and improve your vocabilary,' returned Amy with dignity.

'Don't peck at one another, children. Don't you wish we had the money Papa lost when we were little, Jo? Dear me! How happy and good we'd be, if we had no worries!' said Meg, who could remember better times.

'You said the other day you thought we were a deal happier than the King children, for they were fighting and fretting all the time, in spite of their money.'

'So I did, Beth. Well, I think we are. For though we do have to work, we make fun of ourselves, and are a pretty jolly set, as Jo would say.'

'Jo does use such slang words!' observed Amy, with a reproving look at the long figure stretched on the rug.

Jo immediately sat up, put her hands in her pockets, and began to whistle.

'Don't, Jo. It's so boyish!'

'That's why I do it.'

'I detest rude, unladylike girls!'

'I hate affected, niminy-piminy chits!'

'Birds in their little nests agree,' sang Beth, the peacemaker, with such a funny face that both sharp voices softened to a laugh, and the 'pecking' ended for that time.

'Really, girls, you are both to be blamed,' said Meg, beginning to lecture in her elder-sisterly fashion. 'You are old enough to leave off boyish tricks, and to behave better, Josephine. It didn't matter so much when you were a little girl, but now you are so tall, and turn up your hair, you should remember that you are a young lady.'

'I'm not! And if turning up my hair makes me one, I'll wear it in two tails till I'm twenty,' cried Jo, pulling off her net, and shaking down a chestnut mane. 'I hate to think I've got to grow up, and be Miss March, and wear long gowns, and look as prim as a China aster! It's bad enough to be a girl anyway, when I like boys' games and work and manners! I can't get over my disappointment in not being a boy. And it's worse than ever now, for I'm dying to go and fight with Papa. And I can only stay home and knit, like a poky old woman!'

And Jo shook the blue army sock till the needles rattled like castanets and her ball bounded across the room.

'Poor Jo! It's too bad, but it can't be helped. So you must try to be contented with making your name boyish, and playing brother to us girls,' said Beth, stroking the rough head with a hand that all the dishwashing and dusting in the world could not make ungentle in its touch.

'As for you, Amy,' continued Meg, 'you are altogether too particular and prim. Your airs are funny now, but you'll grow up an affected little goose, if you don't take care. I like your nice manners and refined ways of speaking, when you don't try to be elegant. But your absurd words are as bad as Jo's slang.'

'If Jo is a tomboy and Amy a goose, what am I, please?' asked Beth, ready to share the lecture.

'You're a dear, and nothing else,' answered Meg warmly, and no one contradicted her, for the 'Mouse' was the pet of the family.

As young readers like to know 'how people look', we will take this moment to give them a little sketch of the four sisters, who sat knitting away in the twilight, while the December snow fell quietly without, and the fire crackled cheerfully within. It was a comfortable room, though the carpet was faded and the furniture very plain, for a good picture or two hung on the walls, books filled the recesses, chrysanthemums and Christmas roses bloomed in the windows, and a pleasant atmosphere of home peace pervaded it.

Margaret, the eldest of the four, was sixteen, and very pretty, being plump and fair, with large eyes, plenty of soft brown hair, a sweet mouth, and white hands, of which she was rather vain. Fifteen-year-old Jo was very tall, thin, and brown, and reminded one of a colt, for she never seemed to know what to do with her long limbs, which were very much in her way. She had a decided mouth, a comical nose, and sharp, grey eyes, which appeared to see everything, and were by turns fierce, funny, or thoughtful. Her long, thick hair was her one beauty, but it was usually bundled into a net, to be out of her way. Round shoulders had Jo, big hands and feet, a fly-away look to her clothes and the uncomfortable appearance of a girl who was rapidly shooting up into a woman and didn't like it. Elizabeth, or Beth, as everyone called her, was a rosy, smooth-haired, bright-eyed girl of thirteen, with a shy manner, a timid voice, and a peaceful expression which was seldom disturbed. Her father called her 'Little Miss Tranquillity', and the name suited her excellently, for she seemed to live in a happy world of her own, only venturing out to meet the few whom she trusted and loved. Amy, though the youngest, was a most important person, in her own opinion at least. A regular snow maiden, with blue eyes, and yellow hair curling on her shoulders, pale and slender, and always carrying herself like a young lady mindful of her manners. What the characters of the four sisters were we will leave to be found out.

The clock struck six and, having swept up the hearth, Beth put a pair of slippers down to warm. Somehow the sight of the old shoes had a good effect upon the girls, for Mother was coming, and everyone brightened to welcome her. Meg stopped lecturing and lighted the lamp, Amy got out of the easy chair without being asked, and Jo forgot how tired she was as she sat up to hold the slippers nearer to the blaze.

'They are quite worn out. Marmee must have a new pair.'

'I thought I'd get her some with my dollar,' said Beth.

'No, I shall!' cried Amy.

'I'm the oldest,' began Meg, but Jo cut in with a decided, 'I'm the man of the family now Papa is away, and I shall provide the slippers, for he told me to take special care of Mother while he was gone.'

'I'll tell you what we'll do,' said Beth. 'Let's each get her something for Christmas, and not get anything for ourselves.'

'That's like you, dear! What will we get?' exclaimed Jo.

Everyone thought soberly for a minute, then Meg announced, as if the idea was suggested by the sight of her own pretty hands, 'I shall give her a nice pair of gloves.'

'Army shoes, best to be had,' cried Jo.

'Some handkerchiefs, all hemmed,' said Beth.

'I'll get a little bottle of cologne. She likes it, and it won't cost much, so I'll have some left to buy my pencils,' added Amy.

'How will we give the things?' asked Meg.

'Put them on the table, and bring her in and see her open the bundles. Don't you remember how we used to do on our birthdays?' answered Jo.

'I used to be so frightened when it was my turn to sit in the chair with the crown on, and see you all come marching round to give the presents, with a kiss. I liked the things and the kisses, but it was dreadful to have you sit looking at me while I opened the bundles,' said Beth, who was toasting her face and the bread for tea at the same time.

'Let Marmee think we are getting things for ourselves, and then surprise her. We must go shopping tomorrow afternoon, Meg. There is so much to do about the play for Christmas night,' said Jo, marching up and down, with her hands behind her back and her nose in the air.

'I don't mean to act any more after this time. I'm getting too old for such things,' observed Meg, who was as much a child as ever about 'dressing-up' frolics.

'You won't stop, I know, as long as you can trail round in a white gown with your hair down, and wear gold-paper jewellery. You are the best actress we've got, and there'll be an end of everything if you quit the boards,' said Jo. 'We ought to rehearse tonight.'

'I don't see how you can write and act such splendid things, Jo. You're a regular Shakespeare!' exclaimed Beth, who firmly believed that her sisters were gifted with wonderful genius in all things.

'Not quite,' replied Jo modestly. 'I do think *The Witches' Curse*, an Operatic Tragedy, is rather a nice thing, but I'd like to try MacBETH, if we only had a trapdoor for Banquo. I always wanted to do the killing part. "Is that a dagger that I see before me?"' muttered Jo, rolling her eyes and clutching at the air, as she had seen a famous tragedian do.

'No, it's the toasting fork, with Mother's shoe on it instead of the bread. Beth's stage-struck!' cried Meg, and the rehearsal ended in a general burst of laughter.

'Glad to find you so merry, my girls,' said a cheery voice at the door, and actors and audience turned to welcome a tall, motherly lady with a 'can I help you' look about her which was truly delightful. She was not elegantly dressed, but a noble-looking woman, and the girls thought the grey cloak and unfashionable bonnet covered the most splendid mother in the world.

'Well, dearies, how have you got on today? There was so much to do, getting the boxes ready to go tomorrow, that I didn't come home to dinner. Has anyone called, Beth? How is your cold, Meg? Jo, you look tired to death. Come and kiss me, baby.'

While making these maternal inquiries Mrs March got her wet things off, her warm slippers on and, sitting down in the easy chair, drew Amy to her lap, preparing to enjoy the happiest hour of her busy day. The girls flew about, trying to make things comfortable, each in her own way. Meg arranged the tea table, Jo brought wood and set chairs, dropping, overturning and clattering everything she touched. Beth trotted to and fro between parlour and kitchen, quiet and busy, while Amy gave directions to everyone, as she sat with her hands folded.

As they gathered about the table, Mrs March said, with a particularly happy face, 'I've got a treat for you after supper.'

A quick, bright smile went round like a streak of sunshine. Beth clapped her hands, regardless of the biscuit she held, and Jo tossed up her napkin, crying, 'A letter! A letter! Three cheers for Father!'

'Yes, a nice long letter. He is well, and thinks he shall get through the cold season better than we feared. He sends all sorts of loving wishes for Christmas, and an especial message to you girls,' said Mrs March, patting her pocket as if she had got a treasure there.

'Hurry and get done! Don't stop to quirk your little finger and simper over your plate, Amy,' cried Jo, choking on her tea and dropping her bread, butter side down, on the carpet in her haste to get at the treat.

Beth ate no more, but crept away to sit in her shadowy corner and brood over the delight to come, till the others were ready.

'I think it was so splendid of Father to go as chaplain when he was too old to be drafted, and not strong enough for a soldier,' said Meg warmly.

'Don't I wish I could go as a drummer, a vivan-what's-its-name? Or a nurse, so I could be near him and help him,' exclaimed Jo, with a groan.

'It must be very disagreeable to sleep in a tent, and eat all sorts of bad-tasting things, and drink out of a tin mug,' sighed Amy.

'When will he come home, Marmee?' asked Beth, with a little quiver in her voice.

'Not for many months, dear, unless he is sick. He will stay and do his work faithfully as long as he can, and we won't ask for him back a minute sooner than he can be spared. Now come and hear the letter.'

They all drew to the fire, Mother in the big chair with Beth at her feet, Meg and Amy perched on either arm of the chair, and Jo leaning on the back, where no one would see any sign of emotion if the letter should happen to be touching. Very few letters were written in those hard times that were not touching, especially those which fathers sent home. In this one little was said of the hardships endured, the dangers faced or the homesickness conquered. It was a cheerful, hopeful letter,

full of lively descriptions of camp life, marches and military news, and only at the end did the writer's heart overflow with fatherly love and longing for the little girls at home.

'Give them all of my dear love and a kiss. Tell them I think of them by day, pray for them by night, and find my best comfort in their affection at all times. A year seems very long to wait before I see them, but remind them that while we wait we may all work, so that these hard days need not be wasted. I know they will remember all I said to them, that they will be loving children to you, will do their duty faithfully, fight their bosom enemies bravely and conquer themselves so beautifully that when I come back to them I may be fonder and prouder than ever of my little women.'

Everybody sniffed when they came to that part. Jo wasn't ashamed of the great tear that dropped off the end of her nose, and Amy never minded the rumpling of her curls as she hid her face on her mother's shoulder and sobbed out, 'I am a selfish girl! But I'll truly try to be better, so he mayn't be disappointed in me by and by.'

'We all will,' cried Meg. 'I think too much of my looks and hate to work, but won't any more, if I can help it.'

'I'll try and be what he loves to call me, "a little woman", and not be rough and wild, but do my duty here instead of wanting to be somewhere else,' said Jo, thinking that keeping her temper at home was a much harder task than facing a rebel or two down South.

Beth said nothing, but wiped away her tears with the blue army sock and began to knit with all her might, losing no time in doing the duty that lay nearest her, while she resolved in her quiet little soul to be all that Father hoped to find her when the year brought round the happy coming-home.

Mrs March broke the silence that followed Jo's words, by saying in her cheery voice, 'Do you remember how you used to play Pilgrims Progress when you were little things? Nothing delighted you more than to have me tie my piece bags on your backs for burdens, give you hats and sticks and rolls of paper, and let you travel through the house from the cellar, which was the City of Destruction, up, up, to the housetop, where you had all the lovely things you could collect to make a Celestial City.'

'What fun it was, especially going by the lions, fighting Apollyon and passing through the valley where the hobgoblins were,' said Jo.

'I liked the place where the bundles fell off and tumbled downstairs,' said Meg.

'I don't remember much about it, except that I was afraid of the cellar and the dark entry, and always liked the cake and milk we had up at the top. If I wasn't too old for such things, I'd rather like to play it over again,' said Amy, who began to talk of renouncing childish things at the mature age of twelve.

'We never are too old for this, my dear, because it is a play we are playing all the time in one way or another. Our burdens are here, our road is before us, and the longing for goodness and happiness is the guide that leads us through many troubles and mistakes to the peace which is a true Celestial City. Now, my little pilgrims, suppose you begin again, not in play, but in earnest, and see how far on you can get before Father comes home.'

'Really, Mother? Where are our bundles?' asked Amy, who was a very literal young lady.

'Each of you told what your burden was just now, except Beth. I rather think she hasn't got any,' said her mother.

'Yes, I have. Mine is dishes and dusters, and envying girls with nice pianos, and being afraid of people.'

Beth's bundle was such a funny one that everybody wanted to laugh, but nobody did, for it would have hurt her feelings very much.

'Let us do it,' said Meg thoughtfully. 'It is only another name for trying to be good, and the story may help us, for though we do want to be good, it's hard work and we forget, and don't do our best.'

'We were in the Slough of Despond tonight, and Mother came and pulled us out as Help did in the book. We ought to have our roll of directions, like Christian. What shall we do about that?' asked Jo, delighted with the fancy which lent a little romance to the very dull task of doing her duty.

'Look under your pillows Christmas morning, and you will find your guidebook,' replied Mrs March.

Jo was the first to wake in the grey dawn of Christmas morning. No stockings hung at the fireplace, and for a moment she felt as much disappointed as she did long ago, when her little sock fell down because it was crammed so full of goodies. Then she remembered her mother's promise and, slipping her hand under her pillow, drew out a little crimson-covered book. She knew it very well, for it was that beautiful old story of the best life ever lived, and Jo felt that it was a true guidebook for any pilgrim going on a long journey. She woke Meg with a 'Merry Christmas', and bade her see what was under her pillow. A green-covered book appeared, with the same picture inside, and a few words written by their mother, which made their one present very precious in their eyes. Presently Beth and Amy woke to rummage and find their little books also, one dove-coloured, the other blue, and all sat looking at and talking about them, while the east grew rosy with the coming day.

In spite of her small vanities, Margaret had a sweet and pious nature, which unconsciously influenced her sisters, especially Jo, who loved her very tenderly, and obeyed her because her advice was so gently given.

'Girls,' said Meg seriously, looking from the tumbled head beside her to the two little night-capped ones in the room beyond, 'Mother wants us to read and love and mind these books, and we must begin at once. We used to be faithful about it, but since Father went away and all this war trouble unsettled us, we have neglected many things. You can do as you please, but I shall keep my book on the table here and read a little every morning as soon as I wake, for I know it will do me good and help me through the day.'

Then she opened her new book and began to read. Jo put her arm round her and, leaning cheek to cheek, read also, with the quiet expression so seldom seen on her restless face.

'How good Meg is! Come, Amy, let's do as they do. I'll help you with the hard words, and they'll explain things if we don't understand,' whispered Beth, very much impressed by the pretty books and her sisters' example.

'I'm glad mine is blue,' said Amy, and then the rooms were very still while the pages were softly turned and the winter sunshine crept in to touch the bright heads and serious faces with a Christmas greeting.

'Where is Mother?' asked Meg, as she and Jo ran down to thank her for their gifts, half an hour later.

'Goodness only knows. Some poor creature came a-beggin', and your ma went straight off to see what was needed. There never was such a woman for givin' away vittles and drink, clothes and firin',' replied Hannah, who had lived with the family since Meg was born, and was considered by them all more as a friend than a servant.

'She will be back soon, I think, so fry your cakes, and have everything ready,' said Meg, looking over the presents which were collected in a basket and kept under the sofa, ready to be produced at the proper time. 'Why, where is Amy's bottle of cologne?' she added, as the little flask did not appear.

'She took it out a minute ago, and went off with it to put a ribbon on it, or some such notion,' replied Jo, dancing about the room to take the first stiffness off the new army slippers.

'How nice my handkerchiefs look, don't they? Hannah washed and ironed them for me, and I marked them all myself,' said Beth, looking proudly at the somewhat uneven letters which had cost her such labour.

'Bless the child! She's gone and put 'Mother' on them instead of 'M. March'. How funny!' cried Jo, taking one up.

'Isn't that right? I thought it was better to do it so, because Meg's initials are MM, and I don't want anyone to use these but Marmee,' said Beth, looking troubled.

'It's all right, dear, and a very pretty idea, quite sensible too, for no one can ever mistake now. It will please her very much, I know,' said Meg, with a frown for Jo and a smile for Beth.

'There's Mother. Hide the basket, quick!' cried Jo, as a door slammed and steps sounded in the hall.

Amy came in hastily, and looked rather abashed when she saw her sisters all waiting for her.

'Where have you been, and what are you hiding behind you?' asked Meg, surprised to see, by her hood and cloak, that lazy Amy had been out so early.

'Don't laugh at me, Jo! I didn't mean anyone should know till the time came. I only meant to change the little bottle for a bygone, and I gave all my money to get it, and I'm truly trying not to be selfish any more.'

As she spoke, Amy showed the handsome flask which replaced the cheap one, and looked so earnest and humble in her little effort to forget herself that Meg hugged her on the spot, and Jo pronounced her 'a trump', while Beth ran to the window and picked her finest rose to ornament the stately bottle.

'You see I felt ashamed of my present, after reading and talking about being good this morning, so I ran round the corner and changed it the minute I was up, and I'm so glad, for mine is the handsomest now.'

Another bang of the street door sent the basket under the sofa and the girls to the table, eager for breakfast.

'Merry Christmas, Marmee! Many of them! Thank you for our books. We read some, and mean to every day,' they all cried in chorus.

'Merry Christmas, little daughters! I'm glad you began at once, and hope you will keep on. But I want to say one word before we sit down. Not far away from here lies a poor woman with a little newborn baby. Six children are huddled into one bed to keep from freezing, for they have no fire. There is nothing to eat over there, and the oldest boy came to tell me they were suffering hunger and cold. My girls, will you give them your breakfasts as a Christmas present?'

They were all unusually hungry, having waited nearly an hour, and for a minute no one spoke; only a minute, for Jo exclaimed impetuously, 'I'm so glad you came before we began!'

'May I go and help carry the things to the poor little children?' asked Beth eagerly.

'I shall take the cream and the muffins,' added Amy, heroically giving up the article she most liked.

Meg was already covering the buckwheats, and piling the bread into one big plate.

'I thought you'd do it,' said Mrs March, smiling as if satisfied. 'You shall all go and help me, and when we come back we will have bread and milk for breakfast, and make it up at dinnertime.'

They were soon ready, and the procession set out. Fortunately it was early, and they went through back streets, so few people saw them, and no one laughed at the queer party.

A poor, bare, miserable room it was, with broken windows, no fire, ragged bedclothes, a sick mother, wailing baby and a group of pale, hungry children cuddled under one old quilt, trying to keep warm.

How the big eyes stared and the blue lips smiled as the girls went in.

'*Ach, mein Gott!* It is good angels come to us!' said the poor woman, crying for joy.

'Funny angels in hoods and mittens,' said Jo, and set them to laughing.

In a few minutes it really did seem as if kind spirits had been at work there. Hannah, who had carried wood, made a fire, and stopped up the broken panes with old hats and her own cloak. Mrs March gave the mother tea and gruel, and comforted her with promises of help, while she dressed the little baby as tenderly as if it had been her own. The girls meantime spread the table, set the children round the fire and fed them like so many hungry birds, laughing, talking and trying to understand the funny broken English.

'*Das ist gut! Die Engel-kinder!*' cried the poor things as they ate and warmed their purple hands at the comfortable blaze.

The girls had never been called angel children before, and thought it very agreeable, especially Jo, who had been considered 'Sancho' ever since she was born. That was a very happy breakfast, though they didn't get any of it. And when they went away, leaving comfort behind, I think there were not in all the city four merrier people than the hungry little girls who gave away their breakfasts and contented themselves with bread and milk on Christmas morning.

'That's loving our neighbour better than ourselves, and I like it,' said Meg, as they set out their presents while their mother was upstairs collecting clothes for the poor Hummels.

Not a very splendid show, but there was a great deal of love done up in the few little bundles, and the tall vase of red roses, white chrysanthemums and trailing vines, which stood in the middle, gave quite an elegant air to the table.

'She's coming! Strike up, Beth! Open the door, Amy! Three cheers for Marmee!' cried Jo, prancing about while Meg went to conduct Mother to the seat of honour.

Beth played her gayest march, Amy threw open the door, and Meg enacted escort with great dignity. Mrs March was both surprised and touched, and smiled with her eyes full as she examined her presents and read the little notes which accompanied them. The slippers went on at once, a new handkerchief was slipped into her pocket, well scented with Amy's cologne, the rose was fastened in her bosom, and the nice gloves were pronounced a perfect fit.

There was a good deal of laughing and kissing and explaining, in the simple, loving fashion which makes these home festivals so pleasant at the time, so sweet to remember long afterwards.

NIGHT

18

The Christmas Truce

Published 31st December 1914

in the *New York Times*

FOES IN TRENCHES SWAP PIES FOR WINE

BRITISH AND GERMANS EXCHANGE GIFTS DURING CHRISTMAS TRUCE ON FIRING LINE.

PASS SEASON COMPLIMENTS

ENGLISH SAXON OFFICERS PHOTOGRAPHED TOGETHER BETWEEN THE HOSTILE TRENCHES

Special Cable to the *New York Times*

NORTHERN FRANCE. Dispatch to the
London Daily News.

Serious fighting has been impossible in the region where the British troops are congregated, mainly along the ragged line from Ypres to Armentières and Lille, on account of the shocking state of the country, but there has been an abundance of fun in the sloppy trenches.

A jolly padre who came down from the firing line in the dim, small hours of this morning gave me some amusing little sketches of the celebration of the great festival. On Christmas morning two British soldiers, after signaling truce and good-fellowship from the perilous crown of their trench, walked across to the German line with a plate of mince pies and garniture and seasonable messages. They were most cordially received, had a good 'feed', washed down by a choice bottle of Liebfraumilch, and were sent back with packets of Christmas cards – quite sentimental – wreathed with mistletoe and holly, for distribution among their fellows.

Later in the day the Germans returned the compliment and sent a couple of gayly caparisoned heralds, apparently Landsturm men, across to the evergreen embowered dugouts of the British. An extra-officious soldier promptly arrested them on their appearance within the lines and sat them down in the dampest corner of his trench. Presently an officer came along.

'What in the world have you got there?' said he to the brave British soldier who was guarding his shivering treasures.

'Beggin' your pardon, Sir, a couple of landstreamers, by the look of them. Said they'd come to wish us many happy returns; so I nabbed them, Sir.'

Realising that this was hardly playing the game, the officer read the sentry a little homily on the amenities of the festive season and asked the plump 'landstreamers' to depart with the compliments of the season, to their own lines.

NIGHT

19

In the Week When
Christmas Comes

By Eleanor Farjeon

In the Week When Christmas Comes

By Eleanor Farjeon

This is the week when Christmas comes.

Let every pudding burst with plums,
And every tree bear dolls and drums,
In the week when Christmas comes.

Let every hall have boughs of green,
With berries glowing in between,
In the week when Christmas comes.

Let every doorstep have a song
Sounding the dark street along,
In the week when Christmas comes.

Let every steeple ring a bell
With a joyful tale to tell,
In the week when Christmas comes.

Let every night put forth a star
To show us where the heavens are,
In the week when Christmas comes.

Let every stable have a lamb,
Sleeping warm beside its dam,
In the week when Christmas comes.

This is the week when Christmas comes.

NIGHT

20

Letter to Susy

By Mark Twain

Mark Twain was the pen name of Samuel Clemens.
This is his letter to his daughter Susy.

PALACE OF ST NICHOLAS IN THE MOON
Christmas Morning

My Dear Susy Clemens,

I have received and read all the letters which you and your little sister have written me . . . I can read your and your baby sister's jagged and fantastic marks without any trouble at all. But I had trouble with those letters which you dictated through your mother and the nurses, for I am a foreigner and cannot read English writing well. You will find that I made no mistakes about the things which you and the baby ordered in your own letters — I went down your chimney at midnight when you were asleep and delivered them all myself — and kissed both of you too . . . But . . . there were . . . one or two small orders which I could not fill because we ran out of stock . . .

There was a word or two in your mama's letter which . . .
I took to be 'a trunk full of dolls' clothes.' Is that it? I will call at your
kitchen door about nine o'clock this morning to inquire. But I must not
see anybody and I must not speak to anybody but you.

When the kitchen doorbell rings, George must be blindfolded and
sent to the door. You must tell George he must walk on tiptoe and
not speak — otherwise he will die someday. Then you must go up to
the nursery and stand on a chair or the nurse's bed and put your
ear to the speaking tube that leads down to the kitchen and when
I whistle through it you must speak in the tube and say, 'Welcome,
Santa Claus!'

Then I will ask whether it was a trunk you ordered or not. If you
say it was, I shall ask you what colour you want the trunk to be . . . and
then you must tell me every single thing in detail which you want the
trunk to contain. Then when I say, 'Goodbye and a merry Christmas
to my little Susy Clemens,' you must say, 'Goodbye, good old Santa
Claus, I thank you very much.' Then you must go down into the library
and make George close all the doors that open into the main hall, and
everybody must keep still for a little while. I will go to the moon and
get those things and in a few minutes I will come down the chimney
that belongs to the fireplace that is in the hall — if it is a trunk you
want — because I couldn't get such a thing as a trunk down the nursery
chimney, you know . . .

If I should leave any snow in the hall, you must tell George
to sweep it into the fireplace, for I haven't time to do such things.

George must not use a broom, but a rag – else he will die someday . . . If my boot should leave a stain on the marble, George must not holystone it away. Leave it there always in memory of my visit; and whenever you look at it or show it to anybody you must let it remind you to be a good little girl. Whenever you are naughty and someone points to that mark which your good old Santa Claus's boot made on the marble, what will you say, little sweetheart?

Goodbye for a few minutes, till I come down to the world and ring the kitchen doorbell.

Your loving Santa Claus
Whom people sometimes call 'The Man in the Moon'

Santa Claus

NIGHT

21

A Kidnapped Santa Claus

By L. Frank Baum

A Kidnapped Santa Claus

By L. Frank Baum

Santa Claus lives in the Laughing Valley, where stands the big, rambling castle in which his toys are manufactured. His workmen, selected from the ryls, knooks, pixies and fairies, live with him, and everyone is as busy as can be from one year's end to another.

It is called the Laughing Valley because everything there is happy and gay. The brook chuckles to itself as it leaps rollicking between its

green banks; the wind whistles merrily in the trees; the sunbeams dance lightly over the soft grass, and the violets and wild flowers look smilingly up from their green nests. To laugh one needs to be happy; to be happy one needs to be content. And throughout the Laughing Valley of Santa Claus contentment reigns supreme.

On one side is the mighty Forest of Burzee. At the other side stands the huge mountain that contains the Caves of the Daemons. And between them the valley lies smiling and peaceful.

One would think that our good old Santa Claus, who devotes his days to making children happy, would have no enemies on all the earth; and, as a matter of fact, for a long period of time he encountered nothing but love wherever he might go.

But the daemons who live in the mountain caves grew to hate Santa Claus very much, and all for the simple reason that he made children happy.

The Caves of the Daemons are five in number. A broad pathway leads up to the first cave, which is a finely arched cavern at the foot of the mountain, the entrance being beautifully carved and decorated. In it resides the Daemon of Selfishness. Back of this is another cavern, inhabited by the Daemon of Envy. The cave of the Daemon of Hatred is next in order, and through this one passes to the home of the Daemon of Malice – situated in a dark and fearful cave in the very heart of the mountain. I do not know what lies beyond this. Some say there are terrible pitfalls leading to death and destruction, and this may very well be true. However, from each one of the four caves mentioned there is a small, narrow tunnel leading to the fifth cave – a cosy little room occupied by the Daemon of Repentance. And as the rocky floors of these passages are well worn by the track of passing feet, I judge that many wanderers in the Caves of the Daemons have escaped through the tunnels to the abode of the Daemon of Repentance, who is said to be a pleasant sort of fellow who gladly opens for one a little door admitting you into fresh air and sunshine again.

Well, these Daemons of the Caves, thinking they had great cause to dislike old Santa Claus, held a meeting one day to discuss the matter.

'I'm really getting lonesome,' said the Daemon of Selfishness. 'For Santa Claus distributes so many pretty Christmas gifts to all the children that they become happy and generous, through his example, and keep away from my cave.'

'I'm having the same trouble,' rejoined the Daemon of Envy. 'The little ones seem quite content with Santa Claus, and there are few, indeed, that I can coax to become envious.'

'And that makes it bad for me!' declared the Daemon of Hatred. 'For if no children pass through the Caves of Selfishness and Envy, none can get to *my* cavern.'

'Or to mine,' added the Daemon of Malice.

'For my part,' said the Daemon of Repentance, 'it is easily seen that if children do not visit your caves they have no need to visit mine; so that I am quite as neglected as you are.'

'And all because of this person they call Santa Claus!' exclaimed the Daemon of Envy. 'He is simply ruining our business, and something must be done at once.'

To this they readily agreed; but what to do was another and more difficult matter to settle. They knew that Santa Claus worked all through the year at his castle in the Laughing Valley, preparing the gifts he was to distribute on Christmas Eve, and at first they resolved to try to tempt him into their caves, that they might lead him on to the terrible pitfalls that ended in destruction.

So the very next day, while Santa Claus was busily at work, surrounded by his little band of assistants, the Daemon of Selfishness came to him and said, 'These toys are wonderfully bright and pretty. Why do you not keep them for yourself? It's a pity to give them to those noisy boys and fretful girls, who break and destroy them so quickly.'

'Nonsense!' cried the old greybeard, his bright eyes twinkling merrily as he turned towards the tempting daemon. 'The boys and girls are never so noisy and fretful after receiving my presents, and if I can make them happy for one day in the year I am quite content.'

So the daemon went back to the others, who awaited him in their caves, and said, 'I have failed, for Santa Claus is not at all selfish.'

The following day the Daemon of Envy visited Santa Claus. Said he, 'The toy shops are full of playthings quite as pretty as those you are making. What a shame it is that they should interfere with your business! They make toys by machinery much quicker than you can make them by hand; and they sell them for money, while you get nothing at all for your work.'

But Santa Claus refused to be envious of the toy shops.

'I can supply the little ones but once a year – on Christmas Eve,' he answered, 'for the children are many, and I am but one. And as my work is one of love and kindness I would be ashamed to receive money for my little gifts. But throughout all the year the children must be amused in some way, and so the toy shops are able to bring much happiness to my little friends. I like the toy shops, and am glad to see them prosper.'

In spite of the second rebuff, the Daemon of Hatred thought he would try to influence Santa Claus. So the next day he entered the busy workshop and said, 'Good morning, Santa! I have bad news for you.'

'Then run away, like a good fellow,' answered Santa Claus. 'Bad news is something that should be kept secret and never told.'

'You cannot escape this, however,' declared the daemon, 'for in the world are a good many who do not believe in Santa Claus, and these you are bound to hate bitterly, since they have so wronged you.'

'Stuff and rubbish!' cried Santa.

'And there are others who resent your making children happy and who sneer at you and call you a foolish old rattlepate! You are quite right to hate such base slanderers, and you ought to be revenged upon them for their evil words.'

'But I don't hate 'em!' exclaimed Santa Claus positively. 'Such people do me no real harm, but merely render themselves and their children unhappy. Poor things! I'd much rather help them any day than injure them.'

Indeed, the daemons could not tempt old Santa Claus in any way. On the contrary, he was shrewd enough to see that their object in visiting him was to make mischief and trouble, and his cheery laughter disconcerted the evil ones and showed to them the folly of such an undertaking. So they abandoned honeyed words and determined to use force.

It was well known that no harm can come to Santa Claus while he is in the Laughing Valley, for the fairies and ryls and knooks all protect him. But on Christmas Eve he drives his reindeer out into the big world, carrying a sleighload of toys and pretty gifts to the children; and this was the time and the occasion when his enemies had the best chance to injure him. So the daemons laid their plans and awaited the arrival of Christmas Eve.

The moon shone big and white in the sky, and the snow lay crisp and sparkling on the ground as Santa Claus cracked his whip and sped away out of the valley into the great world beyond. The roomy sleigh was packed full with huge sacks of toys, and as the reindeer dashed onward our jolly old Santa laughed and whistled and sang for very joy. For in all his merry life this was the one day in the year when he was happiest – the day he lovingly bestowed the treasures of his workshop upon the little children.

It would be a busy night for him, he well knew. As he whistled and shouted and cracked his whip again, he reviewed in his mind all the towns and cities and farmhouses where he was expected, and figured that he had just enough presents to go around and make every child happy. The reindeer knew exactly what was expected of them, and dashed along so swiftly that their feet scarcely seemed to touch the snow-covered ground.

Suddenly a strange thing happened: a rope shot through the moonlight and a big noose that was in the end of it settled over the arms and body of Santa Claus and drew tight. Before he could resist or even cry out he was jerked from the seat of the sleigh and tumbled head foremost into a snow bank, while the reindeer rushed onward with the load of toys and carried it quickly out of sight and sound.

Such a surprising experience confused old Santa for a moment, and when he had collected his senses he found that the wicked daemons had pulled him from the snowdrift and bound him tightly with many coils of the stout rope. And then they carried the kidnapped Santa Claus away to their mountain, where they thrust the prisoner into a secret cave and chained him to the rocky wall so that he could not escape.

'Ha ha!' laughed the daemons, rubbing their hands together with cruel glee. 'What will the children do now? How they will cry and scold and storm when they find there are no toys in their stockings and no gifts on their Christmas trees! And what a lot of punishment they will receive from their parents, and how they will flock to our Caves of Selfishness, and Envy, and Hatred, and Malice! We have done a mighty clever thing, we Daemons of the Caves!'

Now it so chanced that on this Christmas Eve the good Santa Claus had taken with him in his sleigh Nuter the Ryl, Peter the Knook, Kilter the Pixie, and a small fairy named Wisk – his four favourite assistants. These little people he had often found very useful in helping him to distribute his gifts to the children, and when their master was so suddenly dragged from the sleigh they were all snugly tucked underneath the seat, where the sharp wind could not reach them.

The tiny immortals knew nothing of the capture of Santa Claus until some time after he had disappeared. But finally they missed his cheery voice, and as their master always sang or whistled on his journeys, the silence warned them that something was wrong.

Little Wisk stuck out his head from underneath the seat and found Santa Claus gone and no one to direct the flight of the reindeer.

'Whoa!' he called out, and the deer obediently slackened speed and came to a halt.

Peter and Nuter and Kilter all jumped upon the seat and looked back over the track made by the sleigh. But Santa Claus had been left miles and miles behind.

'What shall we do?' asked Wisk anxiously, all the mirth and mischief banished from his wee face by this great calamity.

'We must go back at once and find our master,' said Nuter the Ryl, who thought and spoke with much deliberation.

'No, no!' exclaimed Peter the Knook, who, cross and crabbed though he was, might always be depended upon in an emergency. 'If we delay, or go back, there will not be time to get the toys to the children before morning; and that would grieve Santa Claus more than anything else.'

'It is certain that some wicked creatures have captured him,' added Kilter thoughtfully, 'and their object must be to make the children unhappy. So our first duty is to get the toys distributed as carefully as if Santa Claus were himself present. Afterwards we can search for our master and easily secure his freedom.'

This seemed such good and sensible advice that the others at once resolved to adopt it. So Peter the Knook called to the reindeer, and the faithful animals again sprang forward and dashed over hill and valley, through forest and plain, until they came to the houses wherein children lay sleeping and dreaming of the pretty gifts they would find on Christmas morning.

The little immortals had set themselves a difficult task; for although they had assisted Santa Claus on many of his journeys, their master had always directed and guided them and told them exactly what he wished them to do. But now they had to distribute the toys according to their own judgment, and they did not understand children as well as did old Santa. So it is no wonder they made some laughable errors.

Mamie Brown, who wanted a doll, got a drum instead; and a drum is of no use to a girl who loves dolls. And Charlie Smith, who delights to romp and play out of doors, and who wanted some new rubber boots to keep his feet dry, received a sewing box filled with coloured worsteds and threads and needles, which made him so provoked that he thoughtlessly called our dear Santa Claus a fraud.

Had there been many such mistakes the daemons would have accomplished their evil purpose and made the children unhappy. But the little friends of the absent Santa Claus laboured faithfully and intelligently to carry out their master's ideas, and they made fewer errors than might be expected under such unusual circumstances.

And, although they worked as swiftly as possible, day had begun to break before the toys and other presents were all distributed; so for the first time in many years the reindeer trotted into the Laughing Valley, on their return, in broad daylight, with the brilliant sun peeping over the edge of the forest to prove they were far behind their accustomed hours.

Having put the deer in the stable, the little folk began to wonder how they might rescue their master; and they realised they must discover, first of all, what had happened to him and where he was.

So Wisk the Fairy transported himself to the bower of the Fairy Queen, which was located deep in the heart of the Forest of Burzee; and once there, it did not take him long to find out all about the naughty

daemons and how they had kidnapped the good Santa Claus to prevent his making children happy. The Fairy Queen also promised her assistance, and then, fortified by this powerful support, Wisk flew back to where Nuter and Peter and Kilter awaited him, and the four counselled together and laid plans to rescue their master from his enemies.

It is possible that Santa Claus was not as merry as usual during the night that succeeded his capture. For although he had faith in the judgment of his little friends he could not avoid a certain amount of worry, and an anxious look would creep at times into his kind old eyes as he thought of the disappointment that might await his dear little children. And the daemons, who guarded him by turns, one after another, did not neglect to taunt him with contemptuous words in his helpless condition.

When Christmas Day dawned the Daemon of Malice was guarding the prisoner, and his tongue was sharper than that of any of the others.

'The children are waking up, Santa!' he cried. 'They are waking up to find their stockings empty! Ho ho! How they will quarrel, and wail, and stamp their feet in anger! Our caves will be full today, old Santa! Our caves are sure to be full!'

But to this, as to other like taunts, Santa Claus answered nothing. He was much grieved by his capture, it is true; but his courage did not forsake him. And, finding that the prisoner would not reply to his jeers, the Daemon of Malice presently went away, and sent the Daemon of Repentance to take his place.

This last personage was not so disagreeable as the others. He had gentle and refined features, and his voice was soft and pleasant in tone.

'My brother daemons do not trust me overmuch,' said he, as he entered the cavern, 'but it is morning now, and the mischief is done. You cannot visit the children again for another year.'

'That is true,' answered Santa Claus, almost cheerfully; 'Christmas Eve is past, and for the first time in centuries I have not visited my children.'

'The little ones will be greatly disappointed,' murmured the Daemon of Repentance, almost regretfully, 'but that cannot be helped now. Their grief is likely to make the children selfish and envious and hateful, and if they come to the Caves of the Daemons today I shall get a chance to lead some of them to my Cave of Repentance.'

'Do you never repent, yourself?' asked Santa Claus curiously.

'Oh, yes, indeed,' answered the daemon. 'I am even now repenting that I assisted in your capture. Of course it is too late to remedy the evil that has been done; but repentance, you know, can come only after an evil thought or deed, for in the beginning there is nothing to repent of.'

'So I understand,' said Santa Claus. 'Those who avoid evil need never visit your cave.'

'As a rule, that is true,' replied the daemon; 'yet you, who have done no evil, are about to visit my cave at once; for to prove that I sincerely regret my share in your capture I am going to permit you to escape.'

This speech greatly surprised the prisoner, until he reflected that it was just what might be expected of the Daemon of Repentance. The fellow at once busied himself untying the knots that bound Santa Claus and unlocking the chains that fastened him to the wall. Then he led the way through a long tunnel until they both emerged in the Cave of Repentance.

'I hope you will forgive me,' said the daemon pleadingly. 'I am not really a bad person, you know; and I believe I accomplish a great deal of good in the world.'

With this he opened a back door that let in a flood of sunshine, and Santa Claus sniffed the fresh air gratefully.

'I bear no malice,' said he to the daemon, in a gentle voice, 'and I am sure the world would be a dreary place without you. So, good morning, and a merry Christmas to you!'

With these words he stepped out to greet the bright morning, and a moment later he was trudging along, whistling softly to himself, on his way to his home in the Laughing Valley.

Marching over the snow towards the mountain was a vast army, made up of the most curious creatures imaginable. There were numberless knooks from the forest, as rough and crooked in appearance as the gnarled branches of the trees they ministered to. And there were dainty ryls from the fields, each one bearing the emblem of the flower or plant it guarded. Behind these were many ranks of pixies, gnomes and nymphs, and in the rear a thousand beautiful fairies floated along in gorgeous array.

This wonderful army was led by Wisk, Peter, Nuter and Kilter, who had assembled it to rescue Santa Claus from captivity and to punish the daemons who had dared to take him away from his beloved children.

And, although they looked so bright and peaceful, the little immortals were armed with powers that would be very terrible to those who had incurred their anger. Woe to the Daemons of the Caves if this mighty army of vengeance ever met them!

But lo! coming to meet his loyal friends appeared the imposing form of Santa Claus, his white beard floating in the breeze and his bright eyes sparkling with pleasure at this proof of the love and veneration he had inspired in the hearts of the most powerful creatures in existence.

And while they clustered around him and danced with glee at his safe return, he gave them earnest thanks for their support. But Wisk, and Nuter, and Peter, and Kilter he embraced affectionately.

'It is useless to pursue the daemons,' said Santa Claus to the army. 'They have their place in the world, and can never be destroyed. But that is a great pity, nevertheless,' he continued musingly.

So the fairies and knooks and pixies and ryls all escorted the good man to his castle, and there left him to talk over the events of the night with his little assistants.

Wisk had already rendered himself invisible and flown through the big world to see how the children were getting along on this bright Christmas morning; and by the time he returned, Peter had finished telling Santa Claus of how they had distributed the toys.

'We really did very well,' cried the fairy in a pleased voice, 'for I found little unhappiness among the children this morning. Still, you must not get captured again, my dear master; for we might not be so fortunate another time in carrying out your ideas.'

He then related the mistakes that had been made, and which he had not discovered until his tour of inspection. And Santa Claus at once sent him with rubber boots for Charlie Smith, and a doll for Mamie Brown; so that even those two disappointed ones became happy.

As for the wicked Daemons of the Caves, they were filled with anger and chagrin when they found that their clever capture of Santa Claus had come to nought. Indeed, no one on that Christmas Day appeared to be at all selfish, or envious, or hateful. And, realising that while the children's saint had so many powerful friends it was folly to oppose him, the daemons never again attempted to interfere with his journeys on Christmas Eve.

NIGHT

22

Yes, Virginia, There is a Santa Claus

By Francis Pharcellus Church

These letters were printed as an unsigned editorial in the New York Sun *newspaper on 21st September 1897. It has since become history's most reprinted article.*

Dear Editor,

I am 8 years old. Some of my little friends say there is no Santa Claus. Papa says, 'If you see it in THE SUN it's so.' Please tell me the truth; is there a Santa Claus?

Virginia O'Hanlon
115 West ninety-fifth Street

VIRGINIA,

Your little friends are wrong. They have been affected by the skepticism of a skeptical age. They do not believe except they see. They think that nothing can be which is not comprehensible by their little minds. All minds, Virginia, whether they be men's or children's, are little. In this great universe of ours man is a mere insect, an ant, in his intellect, as compared with the boundless world about him, as measured by the intelligence capable of grasping the whole of truth and knowledge.

Yes, VIRGINIA, there is a Santa Claus. He exists as certainly as love and generosity and devotion exist, and you know that they abound and give to your life its highest beauty and joy. Alas! how dreary would be the world if there were no Santa Claus. It would be as dreary as if there were no VIRGINIAS. There would be no childlike faith then, no poetry, no romance to make tolerable this existence. We should have no enjoyment, except in sense and sight. The eternal light with which childhood fills the world would be extinguished.

Not believe in Santa Claus! You might as well not believe in fairies! You might get your papa to hire men to watch in all the chimneys on Christmas Eve to catch Santa Claus, but even if they did not see Santa Claus coming down, what would that prove? Nobody sees Santa

Claus, but that is no sign that there is no Santa Claus. The most real things in the world are those that neither children nor men can see. Did you ever see fairies dancing on the lawn? Of course not, but that's no proof that they are not there. Nobody can conceive or imagine all the wonders there are unseen and unseeable in the world.

You may tear apart the baby's rattle and see what makes the noise inside, but there is a veil covering the unseen world which not the strongest man, nor even the united strength of all the strongest men that ever lived, could tear apart. Only faith, fancy, poetry, love, romance, can push aside that curtain and view and picture the supernal beauty and glory beyond. Is it all real? Ah, VIRGINIA, in all this world there is nothing else real and abiding.

No Santa Claus! Thank God! he lives, and he lives forever. A thousand years from now, Virginia, nay, ten times ten thousand years from now, he will continue to make glad the heart of childhood.

NIGHT

23

The Little Match-Seller

By Hans Christian Andersen

The Little Match-Seller

By Hans Christian Andersen

It was terribly cold and nearly dark on the last evening of the old year, and the snow was falling fast. In the cold and the darkness, a poor little girl, with bare head and naked feet, roamed through the streets. It is true she had on a pair of slippers when she left home, but they were not of much use. They were very large, so large, indeed, that they had belonged to her mother, and the poor little creature had lost them in running across the street to avoid two carriages that were rolling along at a terrible speed. One of the slippers she could not find, and a boy seized upon the other and ran away with it, saying that he could use it as a cradle, when he had children of his own. So the little girl went on with her little naked feet, which were quite red and blue with the cold. In an old apron she carried a number of matches, and had a bundle of them in her hands. No one had bought anything from her the whole day, nor had anyone given her even a penny. Shivering with cold and hunger, she crept along; poor little child, she looked the picture of misery. The snowflakes fell on her long, fair hair, which hung in curls on her shoulders, but she paid them no attention.

Lights were shining from every window, and there was a savoury smell of roast goose, for it was New Year's Eve – yes, she remembered that. In a corner, between two houses, one of which projected beyond the other, she sank down and huddled herself together. She had drawn her little feet under her, but she could not keep off the cold; and she dared not go home, for she had sold no matches, and could not take home even a penny of money. Her father would certainly beat her; besides, it was almost as cold at home as here, for they had only the roof to cover them, through which the wind howled, although the largest holes had been stopped up with straw and rags. Her little hands were almost frozen with the cold.

Ah! Perhaps a burning match might be some good, if she could draw it from the bundle and strike it against the wall, just to warm her fingers. She drew one out – 'scratch!' How it sputtered as it burned!

It gave a warm, bright light, like a little candle, as she held her hand over it. It was really a wonderful light. It seemed to the little girl that she was sitting by a large iron stove with polished brass feet and a brass ornament. How the fire burned! And it seemed so beautifully warm that the child stretched out her feet as if to warm them, when, lo! the flame of the match went out, the stove vanished, and she had only the remains of the half-burnt match in her hand.

She rubbed another match on the wall. It burst into a flame, and where its light fell upon the wall it became as transparent as a veil, and she could see into the room. The table was covered with a snowy white tablecloth, on which stood a splendid dinner service, and a steaming roast goose, stuffed with apples and dried plums. And what was still more wonderful, the goose jumped down from the dish and waddled across the floor, with a knife and fork in its breast, to the little girl. Then the match went out, and there remained nothing but the thick, damp, cold wall before her.

She lighted another match, and then she found herself sitting under a beautiful Christmas tree. It was larger and more beautifully decorated than the one that she had seen through the glass door at the rich merchant's. Thousands of tapers were burning upon the green branches, and coloured pictures, like those in the print shops, looked down upon it all. The little one stretched out her hand towards them, and the match went out.

The Christmas lights rose higher and higher, till they looked to her like the stars in the sky. Then she saw a star fall, leaving behind it a bright streak of fire. Someone is dying, thought the little girl, for her old grandmother, the only one who had ever loved her, and who was now dead, had told her that when a star falls, a soul was going up to God.

She again rubbed a match on the wall, and the light shone round her; in the brightness stood her old grandmother, clear and shining, yet mild and loving in her appearance. 'Grandmother,' cried the little one, 'oh, take me with you. I know you will go away when the match burns out; you will vanish like the warm stove, the roast goose and the large, glorious Christmas tree.' And she made haste to light the whole bundle of matches, for she wished to keep her grandmother there. And the matches glowed with a light that was brighter than the midday sun, and her grandmother had never appeared so large or so beautiful. She took the little girl in her arms, and they both flew upwards in brightness

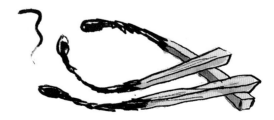

and joy far above the earth, where there was neither cold nor hunger nor pain, for they were with God.

In the dawn of morning there lay the poor little one, with pale cheeks and smiling mouth, leaning against the wall; she had frozen to death on the last evening of the year, and the New Year's sun rose and shone upon a little corpse! The child still sat, in the stiffness of death, holding the matches in her hand, one bundle of which was burnt. 'She tried to warm herself,' said some. No one imagined what beautiful things she had seen, nor into what glory she had entered with her grandmother, on New Year's Day.

NIGHT

24

The Story of the Christ-Child

By Elizabeth Harrison

The Story of the Christ-Child

By Elizabeth Harrison

I want to tell you tonight a story that has been told to little children in Germany for many hundreds of years.

Once upon a time, a long, long time ago, on the night before Christmas, a little child was wandering all alone through the streets of a great city. There were many people on the street, fathers and mothers, sisters and brothers, uncles and aunts, and even grey-haired grandfathers and grandmothers, all of whom were hurrying home with bundles of presents for each other and for their little ones. Fine carriages rolled by, express wagons rattled past, even old carts were pressed into service, and all things seemed in a hurry, and glad with expectation of the coming Christmas morning.

From some of the windows bright lights were already beginning to stream until it was almost as bright as day. But the little child seemed to have no home and wandered about listlessly from street to street. No one took any notice of him, except perhaps Jack Frost, who bit his bare toes and made the ends of his fingers tingle. The North Wind, too, seemed to notice the child, for it blew against him and pierced his ragged garments through and through, causing him to shiver with cold. Home after home he passed, looking with longing eyes through the windows, in upon the glad, happy children, most of whom were helping to trim the Christmas trees for the coming morrow.

'Surely,' said the child to himself, 'where there is so much gladness and happiness, some of it may be for me.' So with timid steps he approached a large and handsome house. Through the windows he could see a tall and stately Christmas tree already lighted. Many presents hung upon it. Its green boughs were trimmed with gold and silver ornaments. Slowly he climbed up the broad steps and gently rapped at the door. It was opened by a large manservant. He had a kindly face, although his voice was deep and gruff. He looked at the little child for a moment, then sadly shook his head and said, 'Go down off the steps. There is no room here for such as you.' He looked sorry as he spoke; possibly he remembered his own little ones at home, and was glad that they were not out in this cold and bitter night. Through the open door a bright light shone, and the warm air,

filled with the fragrance of the Christmas pine, rushed out from the inner room and greeted the little wanderer with a kiss. As the child turned back into the cold and darkness, he wondered why the footman had spoken thus, for surely, thought he, those little children would love to have another companion join them in their joyous Christmas festival. But the little children inside did not even know that he had knocked at the door.

The street grew colder and darker as the child passed on. He went sadly forward, saying to himself, 'Is there no one in all this great city who will share the Christmas with me?' Further and further down the street he wandered, to where the homes were not so large and beautiful. There seemed to be little children inside of nearly all the houses. They were dancing and frolicking about. Christmas trees could be seen in nearly every window, with beautiful dolls and trumpets and picture books, and balls, and tops, and other dainty toys hung upon them. In one window the child noticed a little lamb made of soft white wool. Around its neck was tied a red ribbon. It had evidently been hung on the tree for one of the children. The little stranger stopped before this window and looked long and earnestly at the beautiful things inside, but most of all was he drawn towards the white lamb. At last, creeping up to the windowpane, he gently tapped upon it. A little girl came to the window and looked out into the dark street where the snow had now begun to fall. She saw the child, but she only frowned and shook her head and said, 'Go away and come some other time. We are too busy to take care of you now.' Back into the dark, cold street he turned again. The wind was whirring past him and seemed to say, 'Hurry on, hurry on, we have no time to stop. 'Tis Christmas Eve and everybody is in a hurry tonight.'

Again and again the little child rapped softly at door or windowpane. At each place he was refused admission. One mother feared he might have some ugly disease that her darlings would catch;

another father said he had only enough for his own children, and none to spare for beggar brats. Still another told him to go home where he belonged, and not to trouble other folks.

The hours passed; later grew the night, and colder blew the wind, and darker seemed the street. Further and further the little one wandered. There was scarcely anyone left upon the street by this time, and the few who remained did not seem to see the child, when, suddenly ahead of him, there appeared a bright, single ray of light. It shone through the darkness into the child's eyes. He looked up smilingly and said, 'I will go where the small light beckons; perhaps they will share their Christmas with me.'

Hurrying past all the other houses he soon reached the end of the street and went straight up to the window from which the light was streaming. It was a poor, little, low house, but the child cared not for that. The light seemed still to call him in. From what do you suppose the light came? Nothing but a tallow candle that had been placed in an old cup with a broken handle, in the window, as a glad token of Christmas Eve. There was neither curtain nor shade to the small square window, and as the little child looked in he saw standing upon a neat, wooden table a branch of a Christmas tree. The room was plainly furnished, but it was very clean. Near the fireplace sat a lovely-faced mother with a little two-year-old on her knee and an older child beside her. The two children were looking into their mother's face and listening to a story. She must have been telling them a Christmas story, I think. A few bright coals were burning in the fireplace, and all seemed light and warm within.

The little wanderer crept closer and closer to the windowpane. So sweet was the mother's face, so loving seemed the little children, that at last he took courage and tapped gently, very gently, on the door. The mother stopped talking, the little children looked up. 'What was that, Mother?' asked the little girl at her side.

'I think it was someone tapping on the door,' replied the mother. 'Run as quickly as you can and open it, dear, for it is a bitter cold night to keep anyone waiting in this storm.'

'Oh, Mother, I think it was the bough of the tree tapping against the windowpane,' said the little girl. 'Do please go on with our story.'

Again the little wanderer tapped upon the door. 'My child; my child,' exclaimed the mother, rising, 'that certainly was a rap on the door. Run quickly and open it. No one must be left out in the cold on our beautiful Christmas Eve.'

The child ran to the door and threw it wide open. The mother saw the ragged stranger standing outside, cold and shivering, with bare head and almost bare feet. She held out both hands and drew him into the warm, bright room. 'You poor dear child,' was all she said, and putting her arms around him she drew him close to her breast. 'He is very cold, my children,' she exclaimed. 'We must warm him.'

'And,' added the little girl, 'we must love him and give him some of our Christmas, too.'

'Yes,' said the mother, 'but first let us warm him.'

The mother sat down beside the fire with the child on her lap, and her own two little ones warmed his half-frozen hands in theirs. The mother smoothed his tangled curls, and bending low over his head, kissed the child's face. She gathered the three little ones in her arms and the candle and the firelight shone over them. For a moment the room was very still.

By and by the little girl said softly to her mother, 'May we not light the Christmas tree, and let him see how beautiful it looks?'

'Yes,' said the mother. With that she seated the child on a low stool beside the fire and went herself to fetch the few simple ornaments that from year to year she had saved for her children's Christmas tree. They were soon so busy that they did not notice the room had filled with a strange and brilliant light. They turned and looked at the spot where the little wanderer sat. His ragged clothes had changed to garments white and beautiful. His tangled curls seemed like a halo of golden light about his head, but most glorious of all was his face, which shone with a light so dazzling that they could scarcely look upon it.

In silent wonder they gazed at the child. Their little room seemed to grow larger and larger until it was as wide as the whole world; the roof of their low house seemed to expand and rise, until it reached to the sky.

With a sweet and gentle smile the wonderful child looked upon them for a moment and then slowly rose and floated through the air, above the treetops, beyond the church spire, higher even than the clouds themselves, until he appeared to them to be a shining star in the sky above. At last he disappeared from sight. The astonished children turned in hushed awe to their mother and said in a whisper, 'Oh, Mother, it was the Christ-child, was it not?'

And the mother answered in a low tone, 'Yes.'

And it is said, dear children, that each Christmas Eve the little Christ-child wanders through some town or village, and those who receive him and take him into their homes and hearts have given to them this marvellous vision which is denied to others.

1

2

3

7

8

9

13

14

15

19

20

21

5

6

0

11

12

6

17

18

22

23

24